Limerick County Li

KU-297-056

30012 00684852

NEW YORK
CLASSICS

an C

ACT OF PASSION

GEORGES SIMENON (1903–1989) was born in Liège,
Belgium. He went to work as a reporter at the age of fifteen
and in 1923 moved to Paris, where under various pseudonyms
he became a highly successful and prolific author of pulp
fiction while leading a dazzling social life. In the early 1930s,
Simenon emerged as a writer under his own name, gaining
renown for his detective stories featuring Inspector Maigret.
He also began to write his psychological novels, or *romans
durs*—books in which he displays a sympathetic awareness of
the emotional and spiritual pain underlying the routines of
daily life. Having written nearly two hundred books under his
own name and become the best-selling author in the world,
Simenon retired as a novelist in 1973, devoting himself instead
to dictating several volumes of memoirs.

LOUISE VARÈSE (1891–1989) was an American writer and
translator. In 1969 she was designated a Chevalier de L'Ordre des
Arts et des Lettres by the Republic of France in recognition of her
translations of Baudelaire, Sartre, Proust, Michaux, and Bernanos,
among other writers. She and her husband, the composer Edgard
Varèse, were close friends of Georges Simenon during his years in
the United States, and she translated some fifteen of his novels.

ROGER EBERT has been the film critic of the *Chicago Sun-Times*
since 1967. He won the Pulitzer Prize in 1975. From 1976 through
2006 he co-hosted a weekly film-review program on American
television. He is the author of many books, including the 2011
memoir, *Life Itself*.

OTHER BOOKS BY GEORGES SIMENON
PUBLISHED BY NYRB CLASSICS

WITHDRAWN FROM STOCK

ACT OF PASSION

GEORGES SIMENON

LIMERICK 0006848 52
COUNTY LIBRARY

Translated from the French by
LOUISE VARÈSE

Introduction by
ROGER EBERT

NEW YORK REVIEW BOOKS

New York

THIS IS A NEW YORK REVIEW BOOK
PUBLISHED BY THE NEW YORK REVIEW OF BOOKS
435 Hudson Street, New York, NY 10014
www.nyrb.com

Lettre à Mon Juge/Act of Passion copyright © 1947 Georges Simenon Limited
(a Chorion Limited company); GEORGES SIMENON™ Georges Simenon
Family Rights Limited.
Introduction copyright © 2011 by Roger Ebert
All rights reserved.

Library of Congress Cataloging-in-Publication Data
Simenon, Georges, 1903–1989.
 [Lettre à mon juge. English]
 Act of passion / by Georges Simenon ; introduction by Roger Ebert ; translated
by Louise Varèse.
    p. cm. — (New York Review Books classics)
 ISBN 978-1-59017-385-5 (alk. paper)
 1. Physicians—Fiction. 2. Married men—Fiction. 3. Adultery—Fiction.
 4. Mistresses—Crimes against—Fiction. 5. Psychological fiction. I. Varèse,
Louise, 1890–1989. II. Title.
 PQ2637.I53L413 2011
 843'.912—dc22

                    2010037221

ISBN 978-1-59017-385-5

Printed in the United States of America on acid-free paper.
10 9 8 7 6 5 4 3 2 1

Introduction

I'VE READ more words by Georges Simenon than by any other novelist of the past century. I didn't set out to do that. It wasn't like reading through most of Dickens or Henry James. The books simply accumulated over the decades, and now I have fifty or sixty on my shelf, including all the old Penguin omnibuses. That doesn't include the ones I gave away, lost in hotel rooms, or left behind on airplanes. Before setting out on any significant journey, I always include one Simenon in addition to whatever I am "really reading." I've never started one of his books I didn't finish. I've never been disappointed in one. Some of them (*The Cat*, *Sunday*, *Dirty Snow*, *Tropic Moon*, *The Man Who Watched Trains Go By*) are among my favorite novels, and in them I can see why Paul Theroux has compared Simenon favorably with Camus.

Even the lesser Simenon of the Maigret novels is impressive. Those books are based on a formula—Maigret is confronted by a crime and along with it the particular social milieu in which it has taken place—and essentially they tell the same story over and over again, leading to a sad discovery about some hidden side of human nature. But the sameness of the Maigret stories is nothing like the sameness of the Sherlock Holmes or Travis McGee stories. Simenon isn't concerned with telling stories of those sorts, and his hardly even have plots in the traditional detective-story sense. The conclusion of a Maigret case is more often than not perfunctory, and Maigret mostly resolves his investigations through instinct and intuition, not the police work of his tireless subordinates. He is less like a detective than one of the sad angels in Wim Wenders's *Wings of Desire*, who observe what humans do from a curious and baffled distance of their own.

Simenon's prose style is as pure as running water. I read him in translation, but every translator is clearly responding to the same writer, a writer who seems wary of appearing to write at all. When he found he had written a sentence that called attention to itself, Simenon said, he cut it. The effect is far from artless; the words proceed so calmly and implacably that they seem inevitable, as if they were the fewest needed to make things clear. Simenon's characters speak plainly and directly instead of distinctively. They don't advertise their personalities, and yet the directness gives voice to the complexities that their words seek to suppress and control. A Simenon novel may appear to be all surface, but the depths are always there.

Why is the result so often so moving? Why is there a melancholia in all the books, leavened to a small degree in the Maigret stories by comforting domesticity? Why are there no comedies? No "thrillers"? The same motives over and again: greed, lust, pride, shame? Why is there no sense at the end that justice has been done, or any faith that it can be done? And why, for that matter, are there so many questions, driving the story along? Simenon's questions reflect his own writing process, I believe, as he examines the behavior of the characters under his command. They are questions for which there are no answers. *Act of Passion* is essentially a question posing as an answer. As Charles Alavoine writes his long letter to an examining magistrate, he implies that if the judge could understand him and knew the conditions of his life, it would become clear why he committed murder—why anyone would have. The novel expresses the faith of the narrator that to understand him would be to forgive him. Not to exonerate him—he accepts his guilt—but to understand why he did what he did, and to accept that we might have done the same thing. "You are afraid, to be precise, of what has happened to me," he writes to the magistrate.

You are afraid of yourself, of a certain frenzy which might take possession of you, afraid of the disgust that you feel growing in you with the slow and inexorable growth of a disease.

We are almost identical men, your Honour.

This is not true. Few people are capable of the crimes committed in any Simenon novel, nor does Simenon believe they are. He may have believed he was. He was a man who permitted himself a sexual freedom which would go so far as to what would today be considered rape. If Simenon's characters are capable of theft, adultery, perjury, or murder, did Simenon see himself doing the same kind of thing under similar circumstances? Isn't that question implicit in the work of a man who wrote more than two hundred novels all centered upon transgression?

When Alavoine tells the examining magistrate they are the same man, it raises the question of who the magistrate is. We have only one witness, Alavoine. He portrays the magistrate as a bourgeois professional, like the friends Alavoine used to invite home for an evening of cards. Alavoine in turn depicts himself as an ordinary doctor, a man of fixed routines, a man who submits to the supervision and scrutiny of a mother and a second wife who is like a mother, a man to whom no one could object, and in whom few could take an interest. Alavoine tells us that he is someone "who, for so long, had been only a man without a shadow."

He is a man who has reached middle age having only once done anything which gave him a sharp sense of self. That was the night he spent with a young woman, never named, in Caen: "For the first time I was hungry for a life other than my own." Later he writes: "She was perhaps the first woman I ever loved. For a few hours she gave me the sensation of infinity." Is it possible to love a woman with whom you spend a single night, apparently without learning her name? Alavoine reveals himself as a man who is completely encased within himself, incapable of empathy. If he feels "love" for the girl in Caen, and, as the story develops, for Martine, notice the details he fixes on: the women's shabby cheap possessions, their shared demeanor, their lack of demands, their embodiment of the ordinary. Perhaps what they make him feel most of all is pity for himself: by despising Martine's undemanding capitulation to his desires he is also despising his own docile timidity in his house. What accounts for his insane jealousy of all her lovers past or future? Isn't it rage at their ruling her as easily as he himself has been ruled?

To Alavoine the murder he has committed was inevitable. (It is left to us to wonder if it was, in a sense, suicide.) He expects the judge to find it inevitable too, and perhaps even reasonable. The criminals in Simenon's novels frequently look at their crimes that way. That's what puzzles Maigret in all of his cases, just as it does Simenon. Why are people like that? What shapes them and drives them? How do they lose their moral bearings? In many cases, they are acting because of old wounds and deep hurts. In some, they are helpless in the face of their compulsions. Alavoine, for example, is a fetishist, and like all fetishists he forgives himself his fetish because it seems inescapable. I believe sexual fetishes are formed before the age of conscious choice. I suspect Simenon might agree. The compulsions have been hardwired in early childhood. Most people are lucky to lack fetishes, or to possess socially acceptable ones. Those who do not are out of luck, and those who cannot control them are doomed to transgressive behavior. That this behavior seems profoundly understandable to them, that they accept their desires and forgive themselves for acting on them, is something Simenon confronts us with again and again. People are like that, he says, but why?

Alavoine is obsessed with Martine, the young woman he meets by chance while he is away on a trip and briefly free from his hated home life. Her unremarkable appearance must certainly remind him of his first "love." He describes her slightingly. She has no particular personality. For him she is an object. But he returns again and again to specific details: the way she smokes, the way she sits in a bar, her threadbare appearance, her naïveté and neediness. Martine is so ordinary to Alavoine she is extraordinary. It is possible that if he'd never met her he would never have become a murderer. When he dwells on her, it isn't on her appearance or personality. He is excited by the strength of his own passion. Only once before has he felt so strongly; he didn't know that he still could: he insists on that to the examining magistrate.

I can't remember another novel by Simenon in the first person. Alavoine speaks in the voice that we hear throughout Simenon's work: direct, detached, factual. He doesn't signal his meanings, and it is through his descriptions of places and events that we come to know him. He burdens the magistrate with a great deal of information that has no relevance to his actions, and his eye for specifics is that of a fetishist: he remembers a street, a café, a room, a train, how the light fell—and always the lonely Alavoine is at the center. The accretion of details suggests the mind of a masturbator re-creating scenes of past erotic intensity. It is possible to imagine Alavoine reading over his own pages and feeling aroused. Writing to the magistrate may be his only occasion for a letter that has a more personal purpose.

In his introduction to *Pedigree*, Simenon's longest and most autobiographical novel, Luc Sante refers to Oliver Sacks's essay about a man who "created an accurate three-dimensional map of his native Tuscan village, unseen for many years, from which he could frame and highlight scenes in order to paint them." Sante wonders if Simenon left Belgium "in order to preserve it unchangingly in his head." Certainly Simenon had an inexhaustible memory for places and things, and draws on it effortlessly while never giving the impression of repeating himself. Describing the interior of a brasserie, a shadowy street, someone's clothes, the routine in Alavoine's office, a train platform, the position of shops and houses, Simenon seems to be summoning his own memories and assigning them to Alavoine. Sante writes that he "could make a read of any town and find the plot in its geography." He adds that *Pedigree* is the only novel by Simenon that was "not composed in a willed trance state"—possibly that was a state in which the characters themselves found the setting they needed for what was to happen to them.

Although the Maigret novels are considered inferior to the freestanding books that Simenon called *romans durs*, or hard novels, they contain his method in its pure form. In almost all the books, a crime is committed. In the Maigrets the solution of the mystery is a mystery in its own right, while in the others, the crime reveals itself with a kind of mysterious inevitability. Maigret's method is to assign his officers to investigations and stake-outs of great difficulty, and then remain in his office, or a café, or at Madame Maigret's table, or even in a hotel or hospital room, and ask himself what the criminal could have been thinking. In the course of considering that question, he constructs an image of a person who would think like that, which usually points him toward a suspect, however unlikely. Then Maigret, and the reader of the non-Maigret novels, is left with the question of why a person would think in such a way or do such a thing. For that Simenon has no answer. He was an imperfect man, unfaithful, driven by an unusual appetite for sexual frequency, compelled to write more books than any other great writer ever has. Why did he do that? What made him that way?

—ROGER EBERT

ACT OF PASSION

Chapter One

Monsieur Ernest Coméliau
Examining Magistrate
22 bis Rue de Seine
   Paris (VII)

Your Honour: *

I should like one man, just one, to understand me.
And I would like that man to be you.

We spent many long hours together during all the
weeks of the preliminary investigations. But at that
time it was too soon. You were a judge, you were my
judge, and I would have seemed to be trying to justify
myself. But now you know, don't you, it has nothing
to do with that?

I have no idea what your impression was when you
came into the courtroom – familiar to you, of course.
As for me, how well I remember your arrival! I was
alone between my two guards. It was five o'clock in the
afternoon and the twilight was beginning to gather in
clouds, as it were, around the courtroom.

It was one of the reporters – their table was near the
prisoner's dock – it was a reporter, as I say, first com-

* This letter is addressed to an examining magistrate, whose title
in France is Judge. In French judicial procedure, before the trial, he
extracts from the accused and the witnesses testimony and evidence
which he reports to the magistrate who presides at the trial, but he
does not appear at the trial to prosecute or defend.

plained to his neighbour that it was getting too dark to see clearly. The neighbour spoke to the journalist next to him, a rather sloppily dressed old man with cynical eyes, probably a habitué of the law courts. I don't know whether I am mistaken, but I think he was the one who wrote in his paper that I looked like a toad in ambush.

Perhaps that is why I wonder what impression I made upon you. Our dock – that is, the prisoner's dock – is so low that only the head can be seen above it. It was therefore perfectly natural to keep my chin resting on my hands. I have a wide face, much too wide, which gets shiny easily. But why a toad? To make his readers laugh? Through pure malice? Because he didn't like my looks?

These are minor details, you must excuse me. It is of no importance. The old reporter, whom lawyers and magistrates greet familiarly, gave the Presiding Judge a little sign. The latter leaned over towards the associate judge on his left who, in turn, passed on the message. And thus, finally, the order reached the court attendant who turned on the lights. If I mention this little sideplay, it is because it interested me for quite a while, and reminds me that, when I was a young boy, what fascinated me most at church was to watch the sacristan lighting and extinguishing the candles.

Well, as I said, it was at that moment, with your briefcase under your arm and your hat in your hand, that you slipped in, with an almost apologetic air, among the young law students blocking the entrance. It seems – one of my lawyers sorrowfully told me so – that during most of the trial I behaved very badly. But then, they uttered such stupidities! And with such solemnity! They tell me that I sometimes shrugged my shoulders and even smiled *sarcastically.* An evening paper published a photograph of me taken with a smile on my face during, as he points out, the most pathetic moments in the testimony of one of the witnesses.

'*The hideous smile of the accused.*'

Some people, it is true, speak of Voltaire's hideous smile!

You came in. I had never seen you except behind your desk. You reminded me of the surgeon who comes hurrying into the hospital where his students and assistants are waiting for him.

You did not look in my direction immediately. And yet, what a mad desire I had to greet you, to establish a human contact with you! Is that so ridiculous? Is it cynicism to use the word that was so often employed with reference to me?

We had not seen each other for five weeks. During the two months of the preliminary investigation we had talked with each other almost daily. Do you know, even waiting in the corridor outside your office was a pleasure, and I still sometimes find myself thinking of it nostalgically?

I can still see the line of dark doors to the magistrates' offices as in a monastery – your own door, the benches between the doors, and the floor of the long corridor disappearing in the distance. I was between my two gendarmes, and on the same bench; on other benches sat free men, witnesses, both men and women, and sometimes handcuffed prisoners.

We would sit there staring at one another. That, all that, is what I shall have to explain to you, but I realize that it is an almost impossible task. It would be so much easier if you too had killed!

Just think! For forty years, like you, like everybody else, I was a free man. Nobody dreamed that I should one day become what is called a criminal. In other words I am, in a way, only a criminal by accident.

And yet, when, in your corridor, I watched the witnesses (sometimes people I knew, since they were witnesses in my case), our glances were just about the same as those a man might exchange with a fish.

On the other hand, between those with handcuffs and myself a sort of bond of sympathy was automatically established.

Please don't misunderstand me. I shall probably have to come back to this later on. I have no sympathy for crime, or for murderers. But the others are really too stupid.

Forgive me. That is not exactly what I mean, either.

You came in, and only a short time before, during the recess, after the reading of the interminable indictment – how can a man of good faith collect so many inaccuracies about one of his fellows? – I had heard you discussed.

Indirectly. You know the little room in which the accused wait before the session opens and during the recesses. It is like being backstage at a theatre. But, for me, it brought back memories of the hospital, relatives waiting the outcome of an operation. One passes in front of them – we pass in front of them – talking shop probably, pulling on our rubber gloves after putting out our cigarettes.

'So-and-so? Oh, he's been appointed to Angers ...'

'Didn't he get his degree at Montpellier at the same time as ...?'

I was sitting there on a shiny bench, like the relatives.

Lawyers passed by me, finished their cigarettes, looked at me vaguely without seeing me, as we look at the husband of a patient.

'He's a first-rate fellow, from all accounts. His father was justice of the peace at Caen. He must have married one of the Blanchon girls . . .'

That is the way they were talking about you, as I might have talked a few months before, when we belonged to the same world. At that time, if we had lived in the same city, we would have met a couple of times a week at bridge tables. I would have called you 'My dear Judge' and you would have called me 'My dear Doctor'. Later, as time went on, it would have been:

'Coméliau, old boy.'

'Alavoine, my dear fellow.'

Would we really have become friends? Hearing them talk about you made me ask myself that.

'No, no,' the second lawyer replied. 'You are getting him mixed up with another Coméliau, Jules, his cousin, who was disbarred in Rouen two years ago, and who did marry a Blanchon . . . Our Coméliau married the daughter of a doctor, whose name escapes me . . .'

Another little bond between us.

At La Roche-sur-Yon I count a few magistrates among my friends. I never thought *before* of asking them whether it is the same with their clients as with our patients.

We lived almost six weeks together, if I can put it that way. I know, of course, that during that time you had other problems, other clients, other duties, and that your private life continued. But, just the same, I represented for you, as certain of our patients do for us, the interesting case.

You were trying to understand, I noticed that. Not only with all your professional honesty, but also as a man.

One little detail among others. We were never alone during our interviews, since your stenographer and one of my lawyers, almost always Maître Gabriel, were present. You know your office better than I do, the lofty window with its view of the Seine and the Samaritaine's rooftops like painted scenery, and the door of a closet, almost always ajar, exposing a wash-basin and towels. (I had one just like it in my office where I used to wash my hands between patients.)

Well, in spite of Maître Gabriel's efforts to take first place in everything and everywhere, there were often moments when I had the impression that we were alone and that, by common consent, we had decided that the other two did not count.

Nor was it necessary for us to exchange glances, either. To forget them was enough.

And then those telephone calls! ... Forgive me for mentioning them. It is none of my business, I know. But, after all, didn't you inquire into all the most intimate details of my life, and how can I help being tempted to do the same? Five or six times, almost always at the same hour towards the end of the questioning, you received calls which upset you and made you uncomfortable. As often as you could you answered in monosyllables. You would look at your watch, assuming an air of detachment.

'No ... Not before one o'clock ... It's impossible ... Yes ... No ... Not now ...'

Once, inadvertently, you let slip:

'No child ...'

And you blushed. Then you glanced at me as though I were the only one who counted. To the other two, or rather to Maître Gabriel, you made a commonplace apology.

'Excuse the interruption, Maître ... Where were we ...'

There are so many things that I understood and that you knew I understood! Because, don't you see, I have an enormous advantage over you, no matter what you do, for I have killed.

Let me thank you for having, in your report, summed up the investigation with so much simplicity, with such a total lack of sentimentality that it annoyed the prosecutor until he blurted out that the whole affair, as related by you, sounded more like a simple news item.

You see, I am well informed. I even know that one day when, among magistrates, you were discussing me, they asked you:

'Tell us, since you have had many opportunities of studying Alavoine, what is your opinion – did he act with premeditation or was the crime committed in a moment of uncontrollable passion?'

With what anxiety I would have waited for your answer, had I been there! I would have been on pins and needles wanting to prompt you. It seems that you hesitated, coughed two or three times.

'On my soul and honour, I firmly believe that no matter what Alavoine insists, no matter what he thinks, he acted in a moment when he was not fully responsible, and that his act was not premeditated.'

Well, your Honour, that hurt me. I thought of it again when I saw you among the young law students. There must have been reproach in my eyes, for a little later, when you started to leave, you turned and faced me for several seconds. You raised your eyes. Perhaps I imagined it, but you seemed to be asking pardon.

If I am not mistaken, the sense of that message was: 'I have done my honest best to understand. Henceforth, it is for others to judge you.'

It was the last time we were to see each other. We shall probably never see each other again. Every day new prisoners are brought before you by the gendarmes, fresh witnesses, more or less intelligent or impassioned.

Although I am thankful that it is all over, I must admit that I envy them because they still have a chance to explain, while all I can count on now is this letter, which you will perhaps file away under the heading 'Twaddle', without even reading it.

That, your Honour, would be too bad. I say it without vanity. Not only too bad for me, but too bad for you, because I am going to reveal something which you suspect, something which you don't want to admit and which torments you in secret, something which I know is true, for, since I passed over to the other side, I am more experienced than you: you are afraid.

You are afraid, to be precise, of what has happened to me. You are afraid of yourself, of a certain frenzy which might take possession of you, afraid of the disgust that you feel growing in you with the slow and inexorable growth of a disease.

We are almost identical men, your Honour.

Well then, since I had the courage to go to the bitter end, why not, in turn, have the courage to try to understand me?

As I write, I can see the three lights with green shades hanging over the judges' bench, another over that of the prosecutor and, at the press table, a rather pretty girl-reporter whom a young male colleague, without losing any time, presented with a box of sweets at the second session. She very generously passed it to everyone around her, to the lawyers, to me.

I had one of those sweets in my mouth when you looked in on the trial.

Are you in the habit of looking in at the trials for which you have conducted the investigation? I doubt it. The corridor outside your office is never empty. One prisoner automatically takes the place of another.

And yet twice you came back. You were there when the verdict was read and it is perhaps because of you that I did not fly into a rage.

'What did I tell you!' Maître Gabriel, very proud of himself, exclaimed to his colleagues when they came to congratulate him. 'If my client had been a little more tractable, I'd have won an acquittal . . .'

The imbecile! The smug, cheerful imbecile.

Listen to this. If you want to be amused, here is something to make you laugh. An old lawyer with a beard was bold enough to parry: 'One moment, my dear colleague. With a revolver, yes. Even, at a pinch, with a knife. But with the bare hands, never! An acquittal under such circumstances has never been heard of in the annals of the law.'

With the bare hands! Isn't that magnificent? Isn't that enough to make you want to go over to the other side?

My cell-mate is watching me as I write, without concealing an admiration tinged with annoyance. He is a great strapping boy of twenty-one, a kind of young bull, with a ruddy complexion and candid eyes. He hasn't been in my cell more than a week. Before him there was a poor melancholic fellow who spent all day cracking his finger joints.

My young bull killed an old woman in her little wine shop, hitting her over the head with a bottle, having gone in, as he artlessly put it, to clean up the place.

The judge, it seems, was indignant.

'With a bottle! . . . Aren't you ashamed of yourself?'

And he: 'How could I know she'd be dumb enough to yell? I had to make her stop, and there was the bottle on the counter. I didn't even know if it was full or empty.'

Now he is convinced that I am preparing my appeal, or soliciting some special favour.

What he can't understand, although he too has killed, but accidentally (he's almost right – it was, in a way, the old woman's fault) – what he can't understand is that I myself should insist on proving that I acted with premeditation, in full consciousness of my act.

Do you understand, your Honour? *With premeditation.* Until someone has admitted that, I shall be alone in the world.

In full consciousness of my act!

And, in the end, I'm sure you'll understand, unless, like certain of my colleagues who feel humiliated at seeing a doctor in the prisoner's dock at a murder trial, you prefer to pretend that I am mad, altogether mad, or a little mad – in any case irresponsible or not fully responsible.

They got nothing for their pains, thank God. But even today, when one might suppose that everything had been done, that everything was over, they are still hammering away at it, egged on, I suspect, by my friends, my colleagues, my wife, and my mother.

However that may be, after a month I have not yet been sent to Fontevrault, where I should, theoretically, serve my sentence. They are watching me, I am always being taken to the hospital. They ask a lot of obvious questions that make me smile with pity. The director himself has come several times, spying on me through the peep-hole, and I wonder if they didn't put the young bull in my cell in place of my former melancholy cell-mate to keep me from committing suicide.

It is my calmness that worries them, what the papers called my want of conscience, my cynicism.

I am calm, that's a fact, and this letter should convince you of it. Although I am only a simple family doctor, I have studied enough psychiatry to recognize the letter of a madman.

Too bad, your Honour, if you think the contrary. It would be a great disillusionment to me.

For I still enjoy the illusion of possessing one friend, and that friend, strange as it may seem, is you.

What a lot of things I have to tell you now that I cannot be accused of trying to save my neck and that Maître Gabriel is not there any longer to step on my toes every time I express a truth too simple for him to understand!

We both of us belong to what is called, at home, the liberal professions and what, in certain less advanced milieus, is designated more pretentiously by the term *intelligentsia*. Doesn't the word make you want to laugh? No matter. We belong then to a good middle class, more or less cultivated, the class which furnishes the country with officials, doctors, lawyers, magistrates, quite a few deputies, senators and ministers.

However, from what I have gathered, you are a gener-ation ahead of me. Your father was already a magistrate while mine was still tilling the soil.

Don't tell me that it is of no importance. You would be wrong. You would make me think of the rich who are always saying that money doesn't count in life.

Naturally! Because they have it. But if you don't have any, what then? Have you too ever suffered from the lack of it?

Now take my 'toad's head,' as the witty reporter said. Supposing you had been in my place in the prisoner's dock, he wouldn't have mentioned toads' heads.

One generation more or less makes a difference. You yourself are the proof. Already your face is longer, your skin does not shine, you have the easy manners which my daughters are only now acquiring. Even your glasses, your myopia . . . Even your calm, precise way of wiping the lenses with your little chamois skin . . .

If you had been named magistrate at La Roche-sur-Yon instead of obtaining an appointment in Paris, we should in all probability have become, if not friends, at least friendly acquaintances, as I said before. By the force of circumstances. You would have, I am sure, in all sincerity considered me an equal, but I, deep down, would always have been a little envious of you.

Don't deny it. You have only to look around you. Think of those of your friends who, like me, belong to the first *rising* generation.

Rising where, I wonder. But let that pass.

You were born at Caen and I was born at Bourgneuf-en-Vendée, a village several miles from a little town called La Chataigneraie.

Of Caen I shall have more to say later, for it holds a memory which only recently — since my crime, to use that word — I consider one of the most important of my life.

Why not tell you right away, since it takes us to surroundings you know so well?

I have gone to Caen a dozen times or more, for I have an aunt there, a sister of my father's, who married a man in the china business. You must certainly know his shop on the Rue Saint-Jean, a hundred yards from the Hôtel de France, just where the tram runs so close to the pavement that the pedestrians have to glue themselves against the houses.

Every time I went to Caen it rained. And I liked the rain of your city. I like it for being fine, gentle and silent; I like it for the halo it throws around the landscape, for the mystery with which, in the twilight, it surrounds everybody you meet, especially the women.

Now that I think of it, I remember it was on my first visit to my aunt's. It had just grown dark and everything was shining in the rain. I must have been a little over sixteen. At the corner of the Rue Saint-Jean and another street whose name I've forgotten and which, not having any shops, was completely dark, a girl in a beige raincoat stood waiting, and there were raindrops on the fair hair escaping from under her black beret.

The tram passed, its great yellow eye streaming with water and rows of heads behind the clouded windows. A man, a young man, who was standing on the step, jumped off just in front of the shop with fishing tackle in the window.

After that it was like a dream. At the precise moment he landed on the pavement, the girl's hand caught his arm. And both of them, in a single movement, walked together towards the dark street with such ease that it made one think of the figure of a ballet, and suddenly without a word, on the first doorstep, they glued their bodies together with their wet clothes and their wet skin – and I, too, watching them from a distance, had the taste of a strange saliva in my mouth.

Perhaps because of this memory, three or four years later, when I was already a medical student, I wanted to do exactly the same thing, and in Caen too. As exactly as possible, in any case. But there was no tram and no one was waiting for me.

Naturally, you know the Brasserie Chandivert. For me it's the finest beer-restaurant in France, along with one other in Épinal, where I used to go when I was doing my military service.

There is the illuminated entrance of the cinema to the left. Then the enormous room divided into different parts, the part where you eat, with white tablecloths and silver on the tables, the part where you drink and play cards, and then, at the back, the bottle-green billiard tables under their reflectors, and the almost hieratic poses of the players.

There is also, on the platform, the orchestra, with the musicians in shabby dinner jackets, with long hair and pale faces.

There is the warm light inside and the rain trickling down the window-panes, people who come in shaking their wet clothes, cars stopping outside whose headlights can be seen for an instant.

There are the families dressed in their Sunday best for the occasion, and the habitués, with blotchy red faces, having their game of dominoes or cards, always at the same table, and calling the waiter by his first name.

It is a world, you understand, an almost complete world, a world sufficient to itself, a world into which I plunged with delight and dreamed of never leaving.

You see how far away I was, at twenty, from any criminal court.

I remember that I smoked an enormous pipe which gave me the illusion of being a man and that I looked at all the women with equal avidity.

And then, one evening, what I had always hoped for, without daring to believe it possible, happened. Alone at a table opposite me was a girl, or perhaps a woman, who was wearing a blue tailored suit and a little red hat.

If I knew how to draw I could still make a sketch of her face, her figure. She had a few freckles across her nose and her nose wrinkled when she smiled. And she smiled at me. A sweet friendly smile. Not at all one of those provocative smiles I was more accustomed to.

And we smiled at one another like that for quite a long time, long enough for the audience from the cinema to invade the café during the interval and to leave again when the bell called them back.

Then with her eyes, only with her eyes, she seemed to ask me a question, to ask me why I didn't come and sit beside her. I hesitated. I called the waiter, paid for my drink. Awkwardly I crossed over to her table.

'May I sit down?'

A yes from her eyes – always her eyes.

'You looked so bored,' she said at last when I was seated on the bench.

What we said to each other after that I have forgotten. But I know that I spent one of the happiest, friendliest hours of my life. The orchestra played Viennese waltzes. Outside it was still raining. We knew nothing about one another and I didn't dare to hope for anything.

The movies were over next door. Some people came in and began eating at the table next to ours.

'Let's go . . .' she said simply.

And we left. And outside in the fine rain, which did not seem to bother her, she took my arm in the most natural way in the world.

'Are you staying at a hotel?'

I had told her that I was from the Vendée but was studying at Nantes.

'No, at my aunt's, Rue Saint-Jean . . .'

And then: 'I live quite near the Rue Saint-Jean. Only we must not make a noise. My landlady would put us out.'

We passed in front of my uncle's china shop with its closed shutters, where one sensed a faint glimmer through the glass part of the door, for the room behind the shop was their living-room. My uncle and aunt were waiting up for me. I had no latchkey.

We passed in front of the fishing-tackle shop and I drew my companion down the quiet dark street as far as the first doorstep. You understand why? But when we got there she said: 'Wait till we get to my place . . .'

That is all, your Honour, and telling it I notice that it is ridiculous. She took a key out of her bag. She put a finger on her lips. She whispered in my ear: 'Careful on the stairs . . .'

She led me by the hand along a dark hall. We went up a flight of stairs with creaking boards, and on the first landing we saw a light round the crack of the door.

'Sh . . .'

It was the landlady's room. Sylvia's was next to it. A sordid and rather unsavoury smell floated through the house. There was no electricity and she lit a gas lamp whose light hurt my eyes.

Still whispering, she said before going behind a flowered chintz curtain: 'I'll be back at once. . .'

And I can still see the combs on the stand she used as a dressing-table, the cheap mirror, the bed with a couch cover spread over it.

That's all and it's not all, your Honour. It is all because nothing happened that was not perfectly commonplace. It is not all, because for the first time I was hungry for a life other than my own.

I had no idea who she was or where she came from. I imagined vaguely what kind of a life she led, and felt sure that I was not the first to climb the creaking stairs on tiptoe.

But what difference did it make. She was a woman and I was a man. We were two human beings whispering in that room, in that bed, with the landlady asleep on the other side of the thin wall. Outside it was raining. Outside, from time to time, there were footsteps on the wet pavement, nocturnal voices in the watery air.

My aunt and uncle were waiting for me in the room behind the shop and must have been getting worried.

There was a moment, your Honour, when, with my head between her breasts, I began to cry.

I didn't know why. Do I know today? I began to cry from happiness and from despair, both at the same time.

I held her, simple and relaxed, there in my arms. I remember that she stroked my forehead absently as she stared at the ceiling. I should have liked . . .

And that is what I could not express, what I still cannot express now. Caen, at that moment, represented the whole world. It was there behind the window-panes, behind the wall that hid the sleeping landlady.

All that was the mystery, was the enemy.

But we were two. Two people who didn't know each other. Who had no common interests. Two people whom

LIMERICK
COUNTY LIBRARY
0068485 2

chance had hastily brought together for a moment.

She was perhaps the first woman I ever loved. For a few hours she gave me the sensation of infinity.

She was commonplace, simple and kind. At the Brasserie Chandivert, I had taken her for a young girl waiting for her parents; then for a young wife waiting for her husband.

But, there we were in the same bed, flesh to flesh, doors and windows closed, and there was no one else in the world but the two of us.

I fell asleep. I awoke at dawn and she was breathing peacefully, confidingly, her two breasts uncovered. I was seized with panic on account of my aunt and uncle. I got out of bed without making a sound and I didn't know what I should do, whether to leave money on the dressing-table or not.

I did it shamefacedly. I had my back to her. When I turned round, she was looking at me, and she said softly: 'You'll come back?'

Then: 'Be careful not to wake my landlady ...'

Stupid, isn't it? It took place in your city. Has it happened to you too? As we are about the same age, perhaps you have known Sylvia, perhaps you have ...

As for me, your Honour, she was my first love. But it is only now, after all these years, that I realize it.

And there is something even more serious, you see: I also realize that for twenty years I had been looking for a Sylvia without knowing it.

And that it is after all because of her ...

Excuse me. My bull is furious because they have brought us our dinner and he doesn't dare serve himself before me.

I shall explain all this later, your Honour.

Chapter Two

My mother appeared before the court, for she had been summoned as a witness. Although it seems incredible, I still don't know whether this was done by the prosecution or the defence. Of my two lawyers one of them, Maître Oger, came from La Roche-sur-Yon only to assist his Parisian colleague, and, as it were, to represent my native province. As for Maître Gabriel, he ferociously forbade me to concern myself in any way with my case.

'Is it my job or yours?' he would exclaim in his great gruff voice. 'Just remember, my friend, there isn't a cell in this prison from which I have not extricated at least one client!'

They sent for my mother – perhaps he, perhaps the other side. As soon as the judge pronounced her name, there was a stir in the courtroom; people in the last row and those who were standing behind them stood on tip-toe, and from where I sat I could see them craning their necks.

They reproached me for not having shed a tear, they spoke of my insensibility.

The imbeciles! And what dishonesty, what a lack of understanding, of humanity, to talk in such a way about something they could not possibly know!

Poor Mama. She was dressed in black. For over thirty years she has worn nothing but black from head to foot, like most of our peasant women at home. Knowing her as I do, she must have worried about what she should wear, must have asked my wife s advice. I'd be willing to swear that she repeated at least a dozen times: 'I am so afraid of disgracing him!'

It was certainly my wife who suggested the thin lace collar, so that her clothes would look less like mourning, so that she would not seem to be trying to play on the jury's sympathy.

She was not crying when she came in; you saw that yourself, since you were in the fourth row near the witnesses' entrance. Everything that has been said and written on the subject is false. For years now she has been treated for her eyes, which are always watering. She sees very badly, but refuses to wear glasses, maintaining that you get used to them and keep needing stronger and stronger lenses until finally you go blind. She bumped into a group of young law students who were blocking her passage, and because of this accident it was said that she came in 'staggering with shame and sorrow'.

It was the others who were playing to the gallery, and first of all the judge himself, who half rose from the bench to bow to her with an air of boundless commiseration before turning to the court attendant with the traditional: 'Bring a chair for the witness.'

That crowd holding its breath, those craning necks, those tense faces – all for what? Just to contemplate an unhappy woman, to ask her questions that had not the slightest importance, not even the slightest utility!

'The court, Madam, apologizes for having to inflict such an ordeal upon you, and earnestly requests that you make every effort to remain calm.'

She did not look in my direction. She did not know where I was. She was ashamed. Not ashamed of me, as the reporters wrote, but ashamed of being the target of all those eyes, ashamed of disturbing such important persons, she who had always felt herself of so little account.

For in her mind, you see, and I know my mother well, it was she who was disturbing them. She was afraid to cry. She was afraid to look at anything.

I do not even know what questions they first asked her.

I must insist on this point. I don't know whether other defendants are like me. But for me, I often found it difficult to take an interest in my own trial. Is this due to the fact that the whole farce has so little to do with reality?

Many times during the cross-examination of a witness, or during the frequent verbal clashes between Maître Gabriel and the prosecuting counsel (Maître Gabriel always announced these recurring incidents to the reporters by a premonitory wink), many times, as I say, I suffered lapses which lasted as long as half an hour, during which I watched the faces of the crowd or simply stared at the shadows on the wall in front of me.

Once I started counting the spectators. That took me almost an entire session because I made a mistake and had to begin all over again. There were four hundred and twenty-two persons, including the policemen at the back of the courtroom. Four hundred and twenty-two persons that morning, too, no doubt, staring at my mother whom the judge, at the instigation of Maître Gabriel, asked:

'Your son had meningitis as a child, did he not?'

As though it had been necessary to bring her all the way from the Vendée for that! And from the tone of the question one might have supposed that here was the crux of the whole trial, the key to the enigma. I understood the trick, your Honour. For it was a trick. The two adversaries, the prosecutor and the counsel for the defence, were always asking the witnesses the most asinine questions with an insistence suggesting mysterious designs.

From my bench I could see the jurors scowling and wrinkling up their foreheads, sometimes jotting down notes like detective story readers whom an author, without seeming to do so, has switched on to a new track.

'Yes, sir. He was very sick and I was afraid I was going to lose him.'

'Will you kindly address the gentlemen of the jury. I do not think they heard you.'

And my mother repeating docilely, in exactly the same tone of voice:

'Yes, sir. He was very sick and I was afraid I was going to lose him.'

'Didn't you notice that after his illness your son's character had changed?'

She didn't understand.

'No, sir.'

'Kindly address the gentlemen of the jury.'

It was as great a mystery as that of the Mass, why she should be asked questions in one quarter and have to answer them in another.

'He did not become more violent?'

'He has always been as gentle as a lamb, sir . . .'

'Your Honour . . .'

'. . . Your Honour. At school he would let boys beat him because he was stronger than they were and he didn't want to hurt them.'

Why the smiles in the courtroom and even among the reporters who hastened to jot down her words?

'He was just like a big dog we used to have, who . . .'

Abruptly she fell silent, frightened and confused.

'Dear God,' she must have prayed to herself, 'don't let me shame him . . .'

And still her back was turned towards me.

'After your son's first marriage, you lived with the young couple, did you not?'

'Naturally, your Honour.'

'Face the gentlemen of the jury, they can't hear you very well.'

'Naturally, gentlemen of the jury.'

'Were they happy together?'

'Why shouldn't they have been?'

'You continued to live with your son when he remarried, and you actually still live with his second wife. It would be interesting for the gentlemen of the jury to know whether the relations of the defendant with the latter were the same as those which he enjoyed with his first wife.'

'I beg your pardon?'

Poor Mama who wasn't used to complicated phraseology and who was afraid to admit that she was a little deaf.

'Did your son, if you prefer, behave in the same way with his second wife as with his first?'

The cowards! She was crying now. Not because of me, not because of my crime, but for reasons that were no concern of theirs. And they thought themselves so clever! To look at them, their eyes all glued on a weeping old woman, one would have thought they were about to wrest from her the key of the mystery.

Yet it is perfectly simple, your Honour. With my first wife, who was not a very good housekeeper, who was what they call at home a 'lump of dough', my mother remained the mistress of the house.

With Armande things changed, that was all, because Armande has a stronger personality and very decided tastes of her own. When a woman of sixty is suddenly deprived of her occupations, can no longer give orders to the servants, can no longer fuss over the meals and the children, it is exceedingly painful for her.

That is all. That is why my mother cried. Because she was nothing but a stranger in her daughter-in-law's house.

'Was your son, in your opinion, happy with his second wife?'

'Certainly, sir – excuse me – your Honour.'

'In that case, why did he leave her?'

I did not shed tears, no. I clenched my fists behind my bench, I gritted my teeth. If I hadn't controlled myself I would have jumped up and shouted insults at them.

'If you feel too fatigued to answer any more questions now, we can put them off until the afternoon session.'

'No, your Honour,' Mama stammered. 'I'd rather answer now.'

Then, as the judge turned towards my lawyer, she followed his glance and she saw me. She said nothing. From the movement of her throat I could see that she had swallowed hard. And I know very well what she would have said if she could have spoken to me. She would have asked my forgiveness for bungling so, for being so flustered, so ridiculous. For, she felt ridiculous or, if you prefer, *not in her proper place*, and that, for her, is the worst of all humiliations. She would have asked my pardon for not knowing how to reply and also, perhaps, for shaming me in public.

Maître Oger whom I regarded as a friend, Maître Oger whom my wife had sent up from La Roche to help in my defence so that my city might be associated with it to a certain extent, was guilty of a scurrilous trick. He leaned over and whispered something to Maître Gabriel, who immediately approved with a nod of his head and, like a schoolboy, raised his hand to indicate that he had something he wished to say.

'Your Honour, we, my colleague and I, would like you to ask the witness how her husband met his death.'

'You heard the question, Madam?'

The swine! She had grown so pale that her face looked blue. This and her sudden trembling all over made the court attendant hurry over to her in case she should faint or become hysterical.

'In an accident,' she managed to articulate almost in a whisper.

They made her repeat it.

'What kind of an accident?'

'He was cleaning his gun in the shed behind the house. The gun went off . . .'

'Maître Gabriel?'

'I beg leave to insist, however cruel my question may be. Can the witness affirm to the court that her husband did not commit suicide?'

Indignant, she made an effort to pull herself up proudly.

'My husband's death was accidental.'

All that, you see, your Honour, just to bring one tiny little phrase into the defence, a play for the gallery, for forensic effect. So that Maître Gabriel might exclaim a little later on, pointing to me with a pathetic gesture:

' . . . this man who bears the burden of a cruel heredity . . .'

Cruel heredity! So be it! And yours, your Honour? And that of Maître Gabriel, and of those two rows of jurors whose features I had plenty of time to examine?

A cruel heredity, mine, to be sure, like that of every son of Adam.

The truth, that is what I am going to tell you. Not as it is told in families, for they are ashamed of what they think are taints, but simply as a man, as a doctor, and it will surprise me very much if you don't find points of resemblance with your own family.

I was born in one of those houses over which people begin to grow sentimental even today, and which later, when there are only a few left scattered through the French provinces, will no doubt be turned into museums. An old stone house with vast cool rooms, with unexpected corridors, broken here and there by steps whose *raison d'être* has been forgotten, smelling of wax and the country, of ripening fruit, new-mown hay, and things simmering on the kitchen stove.

This house was formerly, in the time of my grandparents, a manor house, which some people called the château, and it constituted the centre of four farms of over a hundred acres each.

In my father's day there were only two farms. Then later, but long before I was born, only one, and the manor house, in its turn, became a farm; my father began to till the soil himself and to breed animals.

He was a taller, broader and much stronger man than I am. I have been told that at the fairs, when he had been drinking, he was always ready to bet that he could hold a horse on his back, and the old men of the region affirm that he would actually win his wager.

He married late, when he was past forty. He was a good-looking man and still owned enough property to aspire to a rich marriage and so recover his former position.

If you knew Fontenay-le-Comte, about thirty miles from us, you would certainly have heard of the Lanoue girls. There were five of them and an old mother who had been a widow for many years. They had been rich before the death of their father, who had lost his fortune in foolish speculations.

In my father's time the Lanoues, mother and five daughters, still lived in the big house on the Rue Rabelais and even today there are two old-maid sisters, the last of them, still living there.

I truly believe that it would be impossible to find a more absolute or a more dignified poverty than that which existed for years in that household. Their income was so meagre that it allowed hardly more than the shadow of one meal a day, yet this did not prevent the young Lanoue ladies, always accompanied by their mother, from appearing at Mass and at Vespers formally attired in gloves and their Sunday best hats, or from marching home afterwards along the Rue de la République, holding their heads high.

The youngest must have been twenty-five, but it was the thirty-year-old sister whom, one fine day, my father married.

That is my mother. You can understand, your Honour, that the words 'to be happy' have a different meaning for this woman than for the gentlemen of the law.

When she arrived at Bourgneuf she was so anaemic that for several months the stimulating air of the country gave her fits of dizziness. She had a difficult confinement and was not expected to live, hardly surprising considering the fact that I weighed over twelve pounds. I have told you that my father himself cultivated a portion of his land, which is true and yet not altogether true. A large part of the work of our farms consists in 'doing' all the country fairs, and there are fairs in all the market towns of the county as well as in the neighbouring counties.

That was my father's job, as well as organizing rabbit and wild boar hunts when these animals were playing havoc in the region.

My father was, so to speak, born with a gun in his hand. He carried it on his back when he went into the fields. At the tavern he held it between his legs, and I have never seen him when there was not a dog lying at his feet with its muzzle on his boots.

You see that I was not exaggerating when I said that I am closer to the soil than you.

I went to the village school. I fished in the brooks and I climbed the trees like my playmates.

Did I notice at that time that my mother was sad? As a matter of fact, I didn't. For me that gravity which never left her was simply the characteristic of mothers, as well as that gentleness and that smile which seemed always slightly veiled.

As for my father, he would pick me up and swing me on to the back of the work horses or the oxen, would play with me or tease me in language so crude that it would make my mother wince, and his moustache, which I had never known to be anything but grey, always, even in the early morning, reeked of wine or spirits.

My father drank, your Honour. Isn't there invariably one drunkard in every family? In mine, it was my father. He drank at the fairs. He drank at the farmhouses and at the tavern. He drank at home. He would stand in the doorway watching for someone to pass so as to have an excuse to go to the wine-shed with them for a drink.

It was at the fairs that it became dangerous, for when he had drunk, the most hair-raising things seemed to him normal.

I only understood all this later, for I have seen many others like him. I might say that there is one in every village.

A generation separates you from the soil and you have probably never known the unrelenting monotony of the seasons, the weight of the sky on your shoulders from four o'clock in the morning, the passage of the hours with their accumulation of worries.

There are some who don't seem to mind and they are said to be happy. Others drink, do the fairs, and run after the girls. That was my father's case.

As soon as he was awake in the morning he needed a glass of brandy to revive those jovial high spirits for which he was famous throughout the country. Afterwards he needed more glasses, more bottles, to maintain this semblance of optimism. And you see, your Honour, I believe my mother understood that. Who knows, perhaps it is for that reason, more than any other, that I love and respect her.

Never, although most of our time we spent together in the kitchen and, like all children, I kept my ears constantly pricked up, did I hear my mother say:

'You've been drinking again, François.'

Never did she ask my father where he had been, not even on days when there was a fair and he spent the whole proceeds from the sale of a cow on girls.

I firmly believe that, in her mind, that is what she called respect. She respected her man. It was not only gratitude for his having married one of the Lanoue girls. It was simply because she felt that he could not be other than he was.

How often at night, after I had gone to bed, have I heard my father's booming voice announcing the invasion of our house by friends picked up almost anywhere, each one drunker than the other, brought home for a last bottle!

She waited on them. From time to time she would come and listen at my door. And I always pretended to be asleep, for I knew that she was fearful lest I should remember the offensive words being bawled out downstairs.

Every season, or almost, a piece of land was sold, just a splinter, as we say.

'Bah! That bit there, so far away, it gives us more bother than it's worth,' my father would say, but on such days he was not himself.

And he would not touch a drop for days, sometimes weeks, not even a glass of wine. He tried to behave as gaily as usual, but his gaiety was forced.

One day – I can still remember it – when I was playing, near the well, I caught sight of him lying full length at the foot of a haystack with his face turned towards the sky, and he seemed to me so long, so still, that I thought he was dead and I began to cry.

Hearing me, he seemed to come out of a dream. I wonder if he recognized me right away, his eyes had such a faraway look in them.

It was one of those sickly evenings with a sky of a uniform white, at the hour when the grass becomes a sombre green and each blade stands out, shivering in the immensity, as in the paintings of the old Flemish masters.

'What's the matter, sonny?'

'I twisted my ankle running.'

'Come and sit over here.'

I was frightened, but I went and sat down on the grass beside him. He put his arm round my shoulder. We could see the house in the distance and the smoke rising up straight out of the chimney against the white sky. My father was silent, and sometimes I could feel a slight contraction of his hand on my shoulder.

We stared into empty space, both of us. Our eyes must have been the same colour, and I wondered if my father, too, was frightened.

I don't know how long I could have endured that agony, and I must have been very pale, when a gun went off in the direction of the Bois Perdu.

Then my father shook himself, took his pipe out of his pocket and, recovering his normal voice, remarked as he rose:

'That must be Mathieu shooting hares in the Low Meadow.'

Two years went by. I didn't realize that my father was already old, older than the other fathers. More and more frequently he would get up in the night and I could hear the sound of water and voices whispering, and in the morning he would seem tired. At table my mother would push a little cardboard box towards him, saying:

'Don't forget your pill . . .'

Then, one day when I was nine and at school, one of the neighbours, old man Courtois, came into the classroom and spoke to the teacher in a low voice. Both of them looked at me.

'Now, children, I want you to behave yourselves. Alavoine, my boy, will you come out to the courtyard with me?'

It was summer. The cement in the courtyard was hot. There were moss roses around the windows.

'Come here, son . . .'

Old Courtois had already reached the entrance and was leaning against the wrought-iron gate. The teacher put his arm round my shoulder just as my father used to do. The sky was very blue and filled with the song of larks.

'You are a little man now, aren't you, Charles, and I think you love your mama dearly? Well, from now on, you will have to love her even more, because she is going to need you very much.'

Long before he reached the last words, I had understood. And although I had never thought that my father could die, I had a picture of him dead, saw him lying full length at the foot of the haystack as I had seen him that September evening two years before.

I did not cry, your Honour. No more than at the trial. So much for the gentlemen of the press, who would have another chance to call me a slimy toad. I did not cry, but I felt as if I had no more blood in my veins, and when old Courtois, holding me by the hand, took me home with him, I walked on feathers, I went through a universe as weightless as feathers.

They didn't let me see my father. When I got home he was already in his coffin. Everybody who came to the house, where food and drink had to be served from morning to night and from night to morning, everybody kept repeating, as they shook their heads:

'And to think how he loved to hunt and you never saw him without his gun!'

Thirty-five years later a lawyer puffed up with importance and flushed with vanity was to insist upon asking my poor mother:

'Are you sure that your husband did not commit suicide?'

Our peasants of Bourgneuf had more tact. Naturally they gossiped among themselves. But they didn't find it necessary to say anything to my mother.

My father committed suicide. And what of it?

My father drank.

And I, your Honour, am very much tempted to tell you something. But, even with your intelligence, I'm afraid you won't understand.

I won't say that the best men are the ones who drink, but at least they are the ones who have caught a glimpse of something, something they could never attain, something the desire for which has hurt them to the quick, something which perhaps my father and I were staring at that evening when we sat together at the foot of the haystack, our eyes reflecting the colour of the sky.

Think of saying that to the gentlemen of the law and to that snake of a reporter.

I should rather begin telling you about Jeanne, my first wife.

One day at Nantes, when I was twenty-five, solemn personages presented me with my degree of Doctor of Medicine. The same day, after the ceremonies during which I had sweat blood, a gentleman at the door handed me a small box containing a fountain-pen on which my name and the date were engraved in gold letters.

That fountain-pen gave me more pleasure than all the rest. It was the first thing I had ever received for nothing.

You aren't as lucky at the Faculty of Law, your Honour, because you are not as directly connected with certain big industries.

The fountain-pen was given me, as to all the young doctors, by an important pharmaceutical company.

We spent a fairly sordid night celebrating, while my mother, who had been at the ceremony, waited for me in her hotel room. The next morning, without having been to bed, I left with her, not for Bourgneuf, where she had sold almost all the land that was left, but for a little town, Ormois, about twenty kilometres from La Roche-sur-Yon.

That day I think my mother was completely happy. Such a frail little thing, she sat there beside her big son, first in the train, then in the bus. If I had allowed her to, she would have carried the bags.

Would she have preferred it if I had become a priest? It is possible. She had always wanted me to be either a priest or a doctor. I had chosen medicine to please her, when the life of the fields would have suited me so much better.

That very afternoon I began, so to speak, my career as a doctor at Ormois, where my mother had bought the practice of an old doctor who, almost blind, had at last decided to retire.

A wide street. White houses. A square with a church on one side and the town hall on the other. A few old women who still wore the white bonnets of the Vendée.

Finally, since we could not afford a car and since I had to have some sort of a conveyance to take me on my visits to the outlying farms, my mother had bought me a big blue motor-cycle.

The house was sunny and much too big for us, for my mother refused to have a servant and, during my office hours, she herself opened the door for the patients.

The old doctor, whose name was Marchandeau, had

gone to live at the other end of town where he had bought a small house and spent his whole time working in his garden.

He was all grey and wizened, and wore an enormous straw hat that made him look like a queer mushroom. He always stared at people before speaking because of his uncertain eyesight, waiting to hear the sound of their voices.

Perhaps I too was happy, your Honour! I don't know. I was full of goodwill. I have always been full of goodwill. I wanted to please everybody and first of all my mother.

Can you see our little household? She looked after me, spoiled me. All day long she trotted around our unnecessarily large house, trying to make it more and more agreeable, as though she vaguely realized the need for holding me.

Holding me from what? Wasn't it in order to hold me that she wanted me to be a priest or a doctor?

Towards her son she showed the same docility, the same humility as she had always shown towards his father and I hardly ever saw her opposite me at table, for she insisted on waiting on me like a servant.

I was often obliged to jump on to my motor-cycle and go to consult my old colleague, for I felt inexperienced and was sometimes embarrassed by certain cases that came to me.

I wanted to do what was right, you see. I aimed at perfection. Since I was a doctor, I looked upon medicine as a sacred calling.

'Old man Cochin?' Marchandeau would exclaim. 'As long as you stuff him full of twenty francs worth of pills, any old pills, he'll be satisfied.'

For there was no chemist in the village and I myself sold the medicines I prescribed.

'They are all the same. And don't go telling them that a glass of water would do them as much good as a drug. They would lose all confidence in you and, what's more, at the end of the year you would have earned barely enough to pay your licence and your taxes. Drugs, my friend, and more drugs!'

The amusing thing was that as a gardener, old Marchandeau was exactly like the patients he made fun of. From morning to night he treated his borders with the most improbable concoctions which he read about in horticultural catalogues and sent for at great expense.

'Drugs! ... They don't want to be cured, but to be treated ... and whatever you do, don't ever tell them they're not sick ... That'll finish you ...'

Dr Marchandeau, who was a widower, had married off the elder of his two daughters to a chemist in La Roche and lived with the younger one, Jeanne, who was then twenty-two.

I wanted to do what was right, I have told you that, and I repeat it. I don't even know if she was pretty. But I knew that a man, at a certain age, ought to get married.

Why Jeanne? She used to smile at me shyly every time I came to the house. And she it was who served the glass of white wine that is traditional with us. She always wore a discreet, self-effacing air. Everything about her was self-effacing, to such a point that after sixteen years I can scarcely remember what she looked like.

She was gentle, like my mother.

I had no friends in the village. I seldom went to La

Roche-sur-Yon for, in my free moments, I preferred taking my motor-cycle and going off somewhere to fish or to hunt.

I might say that I never really courted her.

'It seems to me,' my mother said one evening as we were waiting for time to go to bed, 'that you're beginning to take quite a fancy to Jeanne.'

'You think so?'

'She's a very nice girl ... No one could say the contrary ...'

One of those young girls, you know, who dons her summer dress and her new hat for the first time Easter Sunday and her winter coat on All Saints' Day.

'Since you won't remain a bachelor all your life ...'

Poor Mama. She would certainly have preferred my being a priest.

It was my mother who married us. We were engaged for almost a year because in the country if you marry too soon, people are sure to say it was a marriage of necessity.

I can still see the Marchandeaus' garden and, in winter, the living-room with its log fire, where the old doctor would promptly fall asleep in his armchair.

Jeanne worked on her trousseau. Then came the moment for deciding about the wedding dress and finally the period when we spent our evenings drawing up and revising the list of guests.

Is that the way you were married, your Honour? I think in the end I began to be a little impatient. When I would kiss her good night at the door I was troubled by the warmth that emanated from her body.

Old Marchandeau was happy to see his last daughter settled.

'Now, at last, I'll be able to live like an old fox ...' he would say in his slightly cracked voice.

We spent three days in Nice, for I was not sufficiently affluent to pay a substitute, and I could not very well leave my patients for any longer than that.

My mother had gained a daughter, a daughter more docile than if she had been her own child. She continued to take charge of the house.

'What shall I do, Mama?' Jeanne would ask with angelic sweetness.

'You must rest, daughter. In your condition ...'

For Jeanne became pregnant right away. I wanted to send her to the hospital at La Roche-sur-Yon for her confinement. I was a little frightened. My father-in-law laughed at me.

'Our midwife here will do the job just as well ... She has brought a good third of the village into the world ...'

It was, nevertheless, a difficult confinement. But my father-in-law continued to encourage me:

'With my wife, the first time, it was even worse. But, you'll see, with the second one ...'

I had always talked about a son, I don't know why. The women – I mean my mother and Jeanne – had set their minds on this idea of a boy.

It turned out to be a girl, and my wife was laid up for three months after the baby was born.

Excuse me, your Honour, if I speak of her in what must seem a somewhat cavalier fashion. The truth is that I did not really know her, that I never knew her.

She was a part of the background of my daily life. A part of the conventions. I was a doctor. I had an office, a cheerful sunny house. I had married a sweet, well-bred young girl. She had just presented me with a child, and I was giving her the best possible care.

In retrospect this seems to me terrible. Because I never tried to know what she thought, to know what she really was.

We slept in the same bed for four years. We spent our evenings together with Mama, sometimes with her father, who would drop in for a nightcap before going to bed.

For me it is a photograph that has already faded. I would not have been in the least indignant if the Judge had pointed a menacing finger at me and said:

'You killed her . . .'

For it is true. Only, in her case, I didn't know it. If I had suddenly been asked:

'Do you love your wife?'

I should have answered with perfect candour:

'But, of course!'

Because it is understood that one loves one's wife. Because that is as far as I could see. It is understood also that one loves one's children. Everyone kept saying:

'The next one will be a fine big boy.'

And I let myself be beguiled by this idea of having a fine big boy. It pleased my mother too.

I killed her because of this idea of having a fine big boy which they had put into my head and which I finally came to believe was my own wish.

When Jeanne had a miscarriage after her first baby, I was a little worried.

'It happens to every woman . . .' her father said. 'You'll see, after you've had a few more years practice . . .'

'She isn't strong . . .'

'Don't you know that the women who seem the most

43

delicate are usually the toughest. Look at your mama . . .'

So I went on. I said to myself that Dr Marchandeau was older than I, had more experience and that in consequence he must be right.

A fine big boy, very big, to the tune of at least twelve pounds, for I weighed twelve pounds when I was born.

Jeanne never said a word. She would follow in my mother's wake around the house.

'Can't I help you, Mama?'

I was out on my big motor-cycle all day, visiting patients, fishing. But I did not drink. I was just barely unfaithful to Jeanne.

We spent the evenings together, the three or the four of us. Then we would go upstairs to bed. I used to say to Jeanne jokingly:

'Shall we make that son tonight?'

She would smile shyly. She was very shy.

She became pregnant again. Everybody was enchanted and predicted the famous twelve-pound boy. As for me, I gave her tonics, hypodermics.

'The midwife is worth more than all those damn surgeons!' my father-in-law kept saying.

When it became necessary to resort to forceps, they sent for me. The sweat poured off my eyelids so that I could hardly see. My father-in-law was there, running back and forth like a little dog who has lost the scent.

'You'll see – everything will be all right . . . ' he kept saying.

Well, I had the child. An enormous baby girl who weighed just under twelve pounds. But the mother died two hours later, without even a look of reproach, murmuring:

'How stupid that I'm not stronger . . .'

44

Chapter Three

During my wife's last pregnancy, I had intercourse with Laurette. If you count at least one drunkard to a village, a 'man who drinks' to every family, is there, I wonder, a single village at home that is without a girl like Laurette?

She worked as chambermaid at the mayor's. She was a good sort, really, and possessed the most amazing frankness, which many people would have called cynicism. Her mother was the priest's housekeeper, but that did not prevent Laurette from going to him to confess her sins.

Shortly after my installation at Ormois, she walked calmly into my office, like an old habitué.

'I just came – I always do, from time to time – to make sure there's nothing the matter with me,' she explained, pulling up her skirts and removing her white drawers, which were stretched across a pair of plump round buttocks. 'Didn't the old doctor tell you about me?'

He had told me about most of his patients but had forgotten, or voluntarily neglected, to mention her. Yet she was one of his regular patients. Of her own accord, her skirt rolled up to her waist, she stretched out on the leather-covered couch I used for my examinations and, with visible satisfaction, pulled up her knees and separated her large milk-white thighs. One felt that she woud have been perfectly happy to keep that pose all day.

Laurette never missed a chance of sleeping with a man.

She confessed that on certain days, when she foresaw this possibility, she went without drawers in order to save time.

'I'm lucky, for it seems I can't have children. But I'm scared to death of catching some filthy disease so I come around regularly for an examination, just to play safe . . .'

I saw her once a month, sometimes oftener. She usually went to confession about the same time. A general house-cleaning, so to speak. Each time she would go through the same motions, would peel off her skin-tight drawers and stretch out on the couch.

I could have had intercourse with her on her very first visit. But instead I spent months desiring her. I would think about it at night in bed. And, with eyes closed, I would take my wife while conjuring up Laurette's broad white thighs. I thought of it so much that I began watching for her visits and once, passing her on the square, I could not help launching, with a nervous laugh:

'So, you don't come to see me any more?'

Why I resisted so long, I don't know. Perhaps because of the exalted idea I entertained of my profession. Perhaps because I was born in fear.

She came. She went through the ritual gestures, watching me with eyes full of curiosity which soon changed to amusement. She was only eighteen, scarcely more than a child herself, yet she looked upon me as a grown person looks upon a child whose thoughts she is able to read.

I was very red and clumsy. I joked nervously:

'Have you had a lot of them lately?'

And I imagined all the men, most of whom I knew, pushing the laughing girl down under them.

'I don't count them, you know. I take things as they come.'

Then, suddenly frowning, as if an idea had just occurred to her:

'Do I disgust you?'

With that, I made up my mind. A second later I was on top of her, like a great animal, and it was the first time that I ever made love to a woman in my office. The first time also that I ever made love to a woman who, although not a professional, was totally without a sense of shame, who was only mindful of her pleasure and of mine, increasing both by every possible means and using the very crudest words.

After Jeanne's death, Laurette continued to come to my office. Later on she came less often, for she became engaged, and to a very nice young fellow at that. But it didn't change her.

Was my mother aware of what was going on between the mayor's chambermaid and myself? Today, I wonder. There are many questions like this which I ask myself now that I am on the other side, not only about my mother, but about almost everybody I have known.

My mother has always moved about noiselessly, as though in church. Except when she went out, I can't remember ever seeing her in anything but bedroom slippers and I have never known any other woman able to come and go as she did, without a sound, without, so to speak, disturbing the air, so that as a small child I was often given a terrible fright when I ran into her, thinking her somewhere else.

'Have you been there all the time?'

How often I have pronounced those words, blushing as I did so!

I don't accuse her of curiosity. I think, however, that she listened at doors, that she has always listened at doors. I even think that, if I told her so, she would not be the least bit ashamed. It is the natural result of the idea she has of her role in life, which is to protect. And in order to protect, one has to know.

Did she know that I slept with Laurette before Jeanne's death? I am not sure. Afterwards, she could not have helped knowing. It is only now, after all this time, that I realize it. I can still hear her anxious voice saying:

'It seems that when she is married, Laurette will go to live at La Rochelle with her husband who intends to open a shop again . . .'

There are so many things that I understand and among them some which frighten me, frighten me all the more because for years I lived without ever suspecting them! Have I really lived? I begin to wonder if I have, to think that I have spent my whole life in a waking dream.

Everything was easy. Everything was regulated. My days followed each other in a slow, even rhythm about which I did not need to bother my head.

Everything was regulated, as I say, everything, except my appetite for women. I don't say for love, but for women. As the doctor of the village, I thought I was bound to be more discreet than other men. I was haunted by the idea of a scandal that would make people point the finger of shame at me and that would create around me in the village a sort of invisible barrier. The sharper and the more painful my sexual desires, the greater the force of my fear, until it even translated itself into childish nightmares.

What frightens me, your Honour, is to think that a woman, my mother, guessed all this.

I began going to La Roche-sur-Yon more and more frequently, for it took no time on my big motor-cycle. I had a few friends there, doctors, lawyers, whom I would meet in a café where there were always two or three women sitting at the back near the bar, and for two years I was obsessed by a desire to sleep with them without ever being able to make up my mind to take them to the nearest hotel.

Coming back to Ormois, I would often ride through all the village streets and all the roads round the village in the hope of meeting Laurette in some unfrequented spot.

That was what I was reduced to, and my mother knew it. With my two little girls to take care of she had, it is true, her hands full. But I am sure it was entirely on my account, and in spite of her horror of having a stranger in her house, that one fine day she decided to take a maid.

I must ask you to forgive me, your Honour, for lingering over these details which very probably seem sordid to you, but, you see, I have the impression that they are extremely important.

Her name was Lucile and she came, of course, from the country. She was seventeen. She was thin and her black hair was always wild. She was so shy that she would drop the plates if I spoke to her unexpectedly.

She rose early, at six o'clock in the morning, and she was the first to go downstairs to light the fire so that my mother could look after my little daughters.

It was in the winter. I can still see the stove smoking, still smell the odour of damp wood which refuses to light, then the aroma of coffee. Almost every morning, inventing some excuse, I would go down to the kitchen – the excuse, for example, of going to gather mushrooms. How many times have I gone out to gather mushrooms in the wet meadows only that I might be alone for a moment

49

LIMERICK
COUNTY LIBRARY

with Lucile, who never dressed until later and had nothing on but a wrapper over her nightgown.

She smelled of bed, warm flannel, and perspiration. I don't think she suspected my designs. On some pretext or other I would manage to rub against her, to touch her.

'Lucile, my poor girl, you are really too thin, you know.'

I had finally found this excuse for feeling her and she, with a pot in her hands, would not protest.

To reach this point took me weeks, months. After that it took weeks longer before I finally got up courage enough to push her over on to the kitchen table, always at six o'clock in the morning while it was still dark outside.

She got no pleasure out of it herself. She was simply glad to make me happy. Afterwards, when she got up, she would bury her head against my chest. Until the day when, at last, she dared raise her head and kiss me.

Who knows? If her mother had not died, if her father had not been left alone on his farm with seven children, had not sent for her to come home and take care of them, perhaps many things would have been different.

It was shortly after this, perhaps two weeks after Lucile left, while instead of a regular maid we had a woman of the neighbourhood who came in by the day to help with the housework, that the incident occurred.

The postmistress had brought her daughter to see me, a young girl about eighteen or nineteen years old who worked in the city and whose health left much to be desired.

'She doesn't eat. She keeps losing weight. She has dizzy spells. I wonder if her employer doesn't work her too hard . . .'

She was a stenographer with an insurance company. I have forgotten her name, but I can see her plainly, more heavily made up than the girls of our region, with enamelled finger-nails, high heels and a headstrong air.

There was nothing really premeditated about it. It is customary in the case of young girls, who often have things to hide from their family, for a doctor to examine them, especially to question them without any witness present.

'We'll just take a look, Madame Blain. If you would like to wait outside for a moment...'

Immediately, I had the impression that the girl was laughing at me and I often wonder if I really had the look of a man haunted by sex. It is possible. I can't help it.

'I'll bet you're going to ask me to get undressed ...'

Just like that, without even giving me the time to open my mouth.

'Oh! It's all the same to me, you know. Anyhow, all doctors are like that, aren't they!'

She took off her dress as though she were in a bedroom, looking at herself in the mirror and afterwards smoothing her hair.

'If you're thinking of tuberculosis, there's no use examining me, I had an X-ray taken last month ...'

Then, finally turning and facing me:

'Shall I take off my slip?'

'That won't be necessary.'

'As you like. What shall I do?'

'Lie down here and don't move...'

'You're going to tickle me ... I warn you I'm terribly ticklish ...'

As I might have expected, the moment I touched her she began to giggle and squirm.

A little bitch, your Honour. I detested her, and I could see her watching me for any tell-tale sign.

'You can't make me believe that doesn't do anything to you. I am perfectly certain that if it were my mother or some other old woman, you wouldn't find it necessary to examine the same places ... If you could only see your eyes ...'

I behaved like an idiot. She was no novice, I had the proof of that. She had noticed an unmistakable sign of the state I was in and it amused her, she was laughing, her mouth wide open. That is what I see most clearly about her: that open mouth and a little pink pointed tongue close to my face. I said, in a strangely unnatural voice:

'Don't move ... Just relax ...'

And suddenly she began to struggle:

'Ah no, I should say not ... you must be crazy! ...'

Another detail I've just remembered, which should have made me more cautious. The cleaning woman was sweeping in the hall behind my office, and from time to time her broom knocked against the door.

Why did I persist when my chances were so slim? In a very loud voice the girl declared:

'If you don't let me go, I'll yell.'

What exactly did the cleaning woman hear? She knocked at the door. She looked in, asking:

'Did you call, Doctor?'

I don't know what she saw. I stammered:

'No, Justine ... Thank you ...'

And when the door closed behind her, the little devil burst out laughing.

'You were frightened, weren't you? Serves you right. I'll get dressed now. What are you going to tell Mama?'

It was my mother who learned of it from Justine. She never mentioned it to me. She gave no sign. But that same evening, or perhaps it was the next day, she remarked in her vague way, as though she were talking to herself:

'I wonder if you haven't made enough money now to think of moving to the city . . .'

And then, which is characteristic of her, following it immediately with:

'After all, we shall have to go to live in the city sooner or later on account of your daughters, for they cannot go to the village school and will have to be sent to the convent . . .'

I had not made a great deal of money, but I had made some, and had put it aside. Thanks to the home pharmacy, as we called it – that is, the latitude allowed country doctors in the matter of selling medicines.

We were prosperous. The bit of land my mother had saved from disaster gave us a small income, without counting the wine, the chestnuts, and the few chickens and rabbits it provided, as well as wood for burning.

'You should make inquiries at La Roche-sur-Yon.'

The truth of the matter is that I had been a widower now for almost two years, and my mother thought it prudent to get me married again. She couldn't eternally hire obliging maids who, one by one, would become engaged or would go to the city where they could earn more money.

'There's no hurry but you might begin thinking about it . . . As for me, you understand, I am happy here and I shall be happy anywhere . . .'

I also think that Mama hated to see me in plus-fours and heavy boots all the time, like my father, spending practically all my free time out hunting.

I was her chick, your Honour, but I was not aware of it. I was a huge chick, six feet tall and weighing two hundred pounds, a monstrous chick, bursting with health and strength and obeying his mother like a little boy.

I am not blaming her. She has worn herself out trying to protect me. She is not the only one.

It even makes me wonder, sometimes, if I wasn't marked with a sign that women – certain women – recognized, and that has made them want to protect me against myself.

That is nonsense, of course. But looking back on one's life one is tempted to say:

'That happened just as if . . .'

There is no question that Mama, after the incident of the little bitch, was frightened. She was well versed in such matters, her husband having been regarded as the most rabid skirt-chaser of the county. How many times would some neighbour come to her saying:

'My poor Clemence, it's your husband again – did you know that he's got the Charreau girl with child?'

For my father was always, quite shamelessly, getting them with child, ready later on, if necessary, to sell another parcel of land. He was not particular, young or old, prostitutes or virgins.

And that, in effect, was the reason for getting me married again.

I have never protested. Not only have I never protested, but I have never been conscious of being held in leash. And that, as you will see, is very important. I am not a rebel, I am just the opposite.

All my life, I think I have told you this many times before and I repeat it, all my life I have wanted to do what was right, simply, calmly, for the satisfaction of duty done.

Does this satisfaction have a bitter after-taste? That is another question. I should rather not answer it right away. Often, towards evening, I have found myself looking up at a colourless sky – a sky washed out, as it were – and thinking of my father lying at the foot of the haystack.

Don't tell me that because he drank and ran after women he was not doing his best. He was doing the best he could, the best allowed him.

As for me, I was only his son. I represented the second generation. As you represent the third. And if I talk about myself in the past tense, it is because, now that I am on the other side, I have gone so far beyond all such contingencies!

For years and years, I did everything that was expected of me, without reluctance, with a minimum of cheating. I was a conscientious country doctor notwithstanding the incident of the little bitch.

And I even think I am a good doctor. When I am with my more learned or more solemn colleagues, I joke or am silent. I don't read the medical reviews. I don't go to medical conventions. Confronted by a disease, I am sometimes embarrassed and I make up an excuse for going into the next room to consult my textbook.

But I have a flair for disease. I hunt it down as a dog hunts down game. I smell it. The very first day I saw you in your office at the Palais de Justice, I ...

You are going to laugh at me. All right! I shall tell you anyhow: look out for your gall bladder! And forgive this sudden professional vanity, or rather, plain vanity. Can't I have a little something left, as I used to say when I was a child.

All the more so, since we are now coming to Armande, my second wife, whom you saw on the witness stand.

She was admirable, everybody said so, and I speak without the least irony. Perhaps, rather too much the 'wife of a La Roche-sur-Yon physician', but one cannot blame her for that.

She is the daughter of what we still call at home a landed proprietor, a man who owns a certain number of farms and who lives in the city on his income. I am not sure if he belongs to the real nobility or if, like most of the country squires of the Vendée, he simply thought fit to add a *de* to his name. In any case, he calls himself Hilaire de Lanusse.

Did you think she was beautiful? I have heard it repeated so often that I no longer know what to think. And I am quite ready to believe it. She is tall, she has a good figure, now on the stout rather than the thin side.

Mothers at La Roche-sur-Yon are always telling their daughters:

'You should learn to walk like Mme Alavoine . . .'

She glides, you noticed that. She moves, as she smiles, with such ease and naturalness that you think it must be a secret.

At the beginning Mama used to say:

'She carries herself like a queen . . .'

You saw what a profound impression she made on the court, on the jury, and even on the reporters. While she was on the stand, I saw people looking me over curiously and it wasn't difficult to guess what they were thinking:

'How could such a lout have a wife like that?'

It is the impression we have always given people, she and I. I should say that it is the impression she has always given me as well, and I have been a long time getting rid of it.

Have I really got rid of it? I shall probably come back to this later on. It is very complex, but I think that I have finally come to understand.

Do you know La Roche-sur-Yon, if only from having passed through it? It is not a real city, not what in France we call a city. Napoleon created it from scratch for strategic reasons, so it lacks that character which the slow contributions of centuries have given to our other cities, the vestiges of numerous generations.

On the other hand, we lack neither space nor sunlight. In fact there's rather too much of both. It is a dazzling city, with white houses along the wide – too wide – boulevards, and right-angle transverse streets eternally swept by breezes.

As monuments, first of all there are the barracks – and they are everywhere. Then the equestrian statue of Napoleon in the centre of the vast esplanade, where men look like ants; the Prefecture, so harmonious in its shady park . . .

That's all, your Honour. One business street to supply the needs of the peasants who come to town for the monthly fairs, a tiny theatre flanked by Doric columns, a post office, a hospital, thirty or so doctors, three or four lawyers, notaries, real estate agents, dealers in farm machinery and fertilizer, and a dozen insurance salesmen.

And two cafés, each with its habitués, opposite the statue of Napoleon and a few steps away from a Palais de Justice with its inner courtyard like a cloister; a few bistros, abounding in good smells, on the market-place, and you've made the rounds of the town ...

We settled down there in May in a house that was practically new, separated from a quiet street by a lawn and clipped hedges. A locksmith came and fastened a handsome brass plate to the iron gate, bearing my name and the information 'General Practitioner' and my office hours.

For the first time we had a formal drawing-room, a real drawing-room with white wainscoting more than shoulder-high and decorative panels over the doors, but it was several months before we could afford to furnish it. Also, for the first time, we had an electric buzzer in the dining-room to ring for the maid.

And this time we engaged a maid right away, for it would have been improper for my mother to be seen doing the housework. Naturally, she did it anyway, but, thanks to the maid, honour was saved.

It is curious that I can scarcely recall that first maid. She must have been very nondescript, neither young nor old. My mother affirms that she was devoted to us and I have no reason for thinking otherwise.

I have a vivid recollection of two enormous lilac bushes covered with blossoms on either side of the iron gateway. Here the patients entered, and their footsteps could be heard on the gravel walk which was indicated by a green arrow and led, not to the main entrance of the house, but to the door of my office, equipped with an electric bell. In this way I was able from my office to count my patients as they arrived, and I must say that for a long time I counted them with a certain anxiety for I was not at all sure of succeeding in the city.

Everything turned out very well. I was satisfied. Of course our old furniture did not suit the new house but that gave us, Mama and me, a subject of conversation, and we would spend evening after evening discussing what we would buy as soon as the money began to come in.

I knew my colleagues before I came to settle there, but only in the way a little country doctor knows the doctors of the district.

We would have to invite them to the house. All my friends said that it was the thing to do. We were both very much frightened, my mother and I, but we nonetheless made up our minds to give a bridge party and to invite at least thirty people.

Does it bore you, perhaps, my telling you all these little details? The house was turned topsy-turvy for several days. I took charge of the wines, liqueurs and cigars; Mama attended to the sandwiches and *petits fours*.

We wondered how many would come, and everybody came, even one extra person, and that person, whom we had never met before, whom we had never heard of before, was Armande.

She came with one of my colleagues, a laryngologist, who had taken upon himself the task of keeping her diverted, for she was a widow who had lost her husband about a year before. Most of my friends at La Roche-sur-Yon were doing the same thing, taking her out in turn, trying to cheer her up.

Was it really necessary? I have no idea. I don't judge anyone. I shall never judge anyone again.

All I knew is that she was dressed in black with touches of mauve and that her blond hair was arranged with exceptional care and formed a heavy and sumptuous mass.

She spoke very little, but she made up for it by looking at everything, seeing everything, especially what she should not have seen, and a little smile would play on her lips, as for example when Mama served tiny little sausages – the caterer had assured her that it was the latest fashion – with our heavy silver forks, instead of sticking them on toothpicks.

It was because of her presence, because of that vague smile which kept playing over her face, that I suddenly became conscious of the emptiness of our house, our few sticks of furniture indiscriminately scattered about now appeared to me absurd, and our voices seemed to reverberate against the walls as in an empty house.

Those walls were almost bare. We had never owned any pictures, we had never thought of buying any. At Bourgneuf our house was decorated with photographic enlargements and calendars. At Ormois I had had framed some of the reproductions published in the art reviews which pharmaceutical companies get out especially for the medical profession.

There were a few of them still hanging on our walls, and it was during this first reception of ours that it occurred to me that my guests, since practically all of them received the same reviews, would recognize them.

It was Armande's smile that opened my eyes. And yet that smile was imbued with the utmost goodwill. Or should I say with an ironic condescension? I have always had a horror of irony and I don't understand it. In any case I felt extremely uncomfortable.

I did not wish to play bridge, for at that time I was not even a middling good player.

'Of course you must,' she said, 'I insist. I want you to be my partner. You'll see, it will go very well ...'

Mama bustled about in agony at the thought of a possible *faux pas*, at the thought that she might shame me. She apologized for everything. She apologized too much, with a humility that was embarrassing. It was obvious that she wasn't used to this sort of thing.

In my whole life I have never played as badly as I did that night. The cards swam before my eyes. I forgot the bids. When it was my lead, I would hesitate, look at my partner, and her smile of encouragement would make me blush all the more.

'Take your time,' she would say. 'Don't let these gentlemen fluster you ...'

There was the matter of the smoked-salmon sandwiches which were much too salty. As we had not tasted them, my mother and I, we fortunately knew nothing about it that evening. But the next day my mother picked up I don't know how many of these sandwiches which had been surreptitiously dropped behind the furniture and curtains.

For several days I kept wondering if Armande had tasted them. I was not in love with her. I never dreamed such a thing possible. The recollection of her simply exasperated me, and I was angry with her for having made me conscious of my clumsiness, if not a lack of breeding. And especially for having done it with that cordial air of hers.

It was the next day at the café where I was in the habit of going almost every evening for an apéritif before dinner that I found out a few details about her life.

Hilaire de Lanusse had four or five children, I don't remember just how many; all of them were married by the time Armande was twenty. She had taken successive courses in singing, dramatic art, music and dancing.

As often happens with the youngest child, a family nucleus no longer existed when she really began to take her place in life and she found herself as free in her father's big house, Place Boildieu, as in a boarding-house.

She had married a musician of Russian origin, who had taken her to Paris, where she lived with him for six or seven years. I know him from his photographs. He was young, with an extraordinarily long narrow face, nostalgic and infinitely sad.

He was tubercular. In order to take him to Switzerland, Armande had claimed her portion of her mother's estate and they lived on this money for another three years, alone in a chalet in the high mountains.

He died there, but it wasn't until several months later that she came back to take her place in her father's house.

I didn't see her again for a week, and if she was often in my thoughts, it was only because her memory was linked to that of our first party, and because in this recollection I looked for the criticism of our behaviour, that of my mother and myself.

One late afternoon when I was having an apéritif at the Café de l'Europe, I saw her through the curtains, walking along the pavement. She was alone. She walked without seeing anyone. She was wearing a black tailored suit, cut with an elegance and a simplicity not often seen in small provincial towns.

I was not in the least moved. I simply remembered the

sandwiches dropped behind the furniture, and the thought was extremely disagreeable.

A few days later at another bridge party given by another doctor, I found myself at the same table with her.

I am not familiar with Paris customs. But at home each doctor, each person belonging to the same milieu, gives at least one bridge party a year, which in the end brings us together two or three times a week at one house or another.

'How are your little girls? I hear you have two adorable little girls.'

Someone had been telling her about me. I was embarrassed, I wondered what they could have said.

She was no longer a girl. She was thirty. She had been married. She knew from experience much more of the world than I, who was a trifle older, and this was perfectly apparent in her slightest remark, in her attitudes, in her way of looking at me.

I had the impression that she was, in a way, taking me under her wing. And she did, indeed, take my part in the bridge game that evening over the question of a finesse I had ventured at random. One of the players was discussing it:

'Admit,' he said, 'that you were lucky. You had forgotten that the ten of spades had been played . . .'

'Not at all, Grandjean,' she declared with her usual serenity. 'The doctor knew it very well. The proof is that in the previous trick he discarded a heart, which he would never have done otherwise.'

It wasn't true. She knew that I knew it. And I knew that she knew.

Do you understand what that meant?

A short time after this, when we had met not more than four times in all, my elder daughter Anne-Marie went down with diphtheria. My daughters, like most doctor's children, acquired during their childhood every one of the infectious diseases.

I was unwilling to send her to the city hospital, which at that time I did not consider up to standard. There was not a bed available in any of the private hospitals.

I decided to quarantine Anne-Marie at home and, as I did not want to take the responsibility myself, I called in my friend the laryngologist.

Dambois, that's his name. With what passionate interest he must have read all the newspaper accounts of my trial! He is very tall and thin, with an excessively long neck, a prominent Adam's apple, and the eyes of a clown.

'What we'll have to find first of all,' he said, 'is a nurse. I'll do some telephoning in a minute, but I very much doubt if I'll succeed . . .'

There was an epidemic of diphtheria throughout the Department and it was not even easy to get serum.

'In any case, it is out of the question for your mother to continue to nurse our little patient and to take care of your younger daughter at the same time. I don't know just what I am going to do, but I'll take care of it. Don't you worry, old man . . .'

I was in a state of collapse. I was frightened. I didn't know what I was doing. To tell the truth, I left everything to Dambois, I had no will of my own left.

'Hello! . . . Is that you, Alavoine? . . . This is Dambois . . .' It was hardly half an hour since he had left the house.

'At last I've found a solution. As I thought, not a nurse

64

to be had, not even at Nantes, where the epidemic is even worse than here ... Armande, who overheard me telephoning, has offered of her own accord to nurse your daughter ... She is used to sickness ... She is intelligent ... She has the necessary patience ... She will be at your house in an hour or two ... Just set up a camp bed for her in our little patient's room ... Not at all, old man, it's no trouble to her at all ... quite the contrary ... Between ourselves, I confess I'm delighted, it will be something to occupy her mind ... You don't know her ... People imagine because she is always smiling that she got over it ... My wife and I, who see her every day, who know her intimately, we realize that she is completely demoralized, and, I tell you this confidentially, for a long time we thought it would finish badly ... So no scruples ...

'If you really want to put her at her ease, you will treat her like an ordinary nurse, pay no attention to her, and show her that you have confidence in her as far as the patient is concerned ...

'I'll hang up, old man, because she's downstairs now, waiting for your answer before going home to pack her bag ... She'll be at your house in an hour or two ...

'She likes you very much ... But it's true ... only she doesn't show her feelings readily ...

'We'll have the serum tomorrow evening. Go back to your patients and leave the rest to us ...'

That, your Honour, is how Armande entered our house, a little travelling bag in her hand. The first thing she did was to put on a white hospital coat and tie a kerchief over her fair hair.

'And now, Mme Alavoine,' she said to Mama, 'under no consideration must you enter the sick-room. You know it is a question of the health of your other little girl. I have brought an electric stove with me and everything I shall need. You don't have to bother about a thing . . .'

A few moments later I found Mama in tears in the hall outside the kitchen. She didn't want to cry in front of the maid – nor in front of me.

'What's the matter?'

'Nothing,' she replied, blowing her nose.

'Anne-Marie will be well taken care of . . .'

'Yes . . .'

'Dambois assures me that she is in no danger and he wouldn't say so if he had the slightest doubt . . .'

'I know . . .'

'Then why are you crying?'

'I'm not crying . . .'

Poor Mama, she knew very well that what had entered our house was a will stronger than her own, to which she would have to yield.

Another thing, your Honour. You are going to say that I accumulate the most ridiculous details. But do you know what, in my opinion, was the most painful thing of all for my mother? The electric stove which the *other woman* had had the foresight to bring with her.

The *other woman* had thought of everything, you understand? She needed no one. She refused to need anyone.

Chapter Four

It happened the second night. She probably knocked on my door but did not wait for an answer. Without turning on the electric switch and, as though familiar with the room, she came over and lighted the lamp by my bed. I was vaguely conscious of someone touching my shoulder. I sleep heavily. My hair at nights gets plastered down over my skull and makes my face look even broader than usual. I am always too hot, and my face must have been shiny.

When I opened my eyes she was seated on the edge of my bed in her white hospital coat, her kerchief on her head, and calm and serene, began by saying:

'Don't be frightened, Charles. I simply wanted to talk to you.'

There were little mouse-like noises in the house – my mother probably, for she hardly slept at all and must have been on the alert.

That was the first time Armande ever called me Charles. It is true, she had lived where a certain familiarity comes naturally.

'Anne-Marie is not worse, so don't worry . . .'

She had no dress on under her hospital coat, only her lingerie, so that in places the material seemed moulded to her flesh.

'Henri is certainly an excellent physician,' she went on, 'and I should not like to hurt his feelings. I talked to him seriously a little while ago, but he does not seem to understand. You see, in medicine he is inclined to be over-cautious, and in this case, you being a colleague, he feels his responsibility all the more.'

I would have given a good deal to run a comb through my hair and rinse my mouth. I was obliged to keep under the covers on account of my wrinkled pyjamas. She thought of handing me a glass of water, and proposed:

'A cigarette?'

She lighted one too.

'In Switzerland I happened to nurse a case similar to Anne-Marie's, the daughter of one of my neighbours. That will explain why I know something about it. Besides we had many friends who were doctors, and we used to spend night after night discussing medical questions ...'

My mother must have been frightened. I saw her standing there framed in the open doorway, grey all over, lighter than the darkness of the hall beyond. She was wearing a wrapper, and her hair was done up in curlers.

'Don't be uneasy, Mme Alavoine. I simply wanted to consult your son as to how the treatment should be applied ...'

Mama looked at our two cigarettes with their smoke mingling in a luminous halo around the bedside lamp. I am sure this is what struck her most forcibly. We were smoking cigarettes – together, at three o'clock in the morning, on my bed.

'I didn't know, excuse me. I heard a noise and I came to see ...'

She disappeared, and Armande continued as if we had never been interrupted:

'Well, Henri gave her twenty thousand units of serum.

I did not like to interfere. But you saw what the temperature was this evening?'

'Let's go down to my office,' I said.

She turned her back while I put on my dressing-gown. Once I was on more solid ground, I filled my pipe, which restored a little of my self-assurance.

'What was it tonight?'

'A hundred and four. That is why I woke you. Most professors I've known have very different ideas about serum from Henri's. One of them used to tell us over and over again: strike hard, or don't strike at all; a massive dose, or nothing . . .'

For three years, at Nantes, I had heard my old master Chevalier, in his ringing voice, say the same thing, only he, with his legendary brutality, would add:

'If the patient croaks, that's his fault.'

I noticed that two or three of my books on therapeutics were missing from the shelves and I knew that Armande must have come down and taken them. For ten minutes she talked about diphtheria in a way I should have been incapable of doing myself.

'You can, of course, telephone Dr Dambois. But I wonder if it wouldn't be simpler and less galling for him if you simply took it upon yourself to give her another injection.'

This was an extremely grave problem. There was my daughter to be considered. On the other hand it was a question of a colleague, of a heavy professional responsibility, of what must really be termed an indelicacy, to say the least.

'Come and take a look . . .'

My daughter's room was already her domain, organized to suit herself. Why did one feel it the moment one entered? And why, in spite of the scent of illness and medicines, was it her scent that struck me, although the cot was still undisturbed?

'Read this passage ... You will see that almost all the great specialists are of the same opinion.'

That night, your Honour, I wonder if I wasn't criminal at heart? I yielded. I did what she had decided I should do. Not because I believed it was the right thing to do, not because of my master Chevalier's opinions on the subject of serums, or because of the texts I was given to read.

I yielded because she willed me to.

I was fully aware of it. My daughter's life was at stake. If only from the strict point of view of ethics, I was committing a grave dereliction.

I did it and I knew I was doing wrong. I knew it so well that I trembled at the thought of seeing the phantom-like figure of my mother reappear.

Ten thousand units more. She helped me give the hypodermic. Actually she left me nothing but the final gesture to accomplish. During the operation her hair brushed against my cheek.

It did not affect me. I did not desire her and I think I already felt certain that I would never desire her.

'Now go back to bed. You begin seeing your patients at eight o'clock.'

I slept badly. In my semi-consciousness I had the sensation of something inescapable. Don't think I am inventing in retrospect. Besides I was pleased, in a way, in spite of my distress and uneasiness. I told myself:

'It has nothing to do with me. It's her doing.'

Finally I fell asleep. When I came downstairs next

morning I found Armande in the garden, where she had gone for a breath of fresh air, and she was now wearing a dress under her white coat.

'A hundred and two and one tenth,' she cried joyously. 'She perspired so much early this morning that twice I had to change her sheets.'

Neither of us said anything to Dambois. Armande did not find it difficult to keep silent. But I had to bite my tongue every time I saw him.

I was about to write, your Honour, that what I have just told you is the entire story of our marriage. She entered our house without my asking, without my wanting her to. It was she who on the second day made – or forced me to make – capital decisions.

After she came, Mama was transformed into a grey frightened little mouse who glided past the doors, and she resumed her old habit of apologizing for everything and nothing.

And yet, at the beginning, Armande had Mama on her side. From having seen her on the witness-stand, you only saw the woman of forty. Ten years ago, she possessed the same self-assurance, the same innate faculty for dominating and orchestrating, as I call it, everything around her without seeming to. With, at that time, something a little more resilient about her than today, not only physically, but morally.

It was to her the maid went for orders as a matter of course, reiterating a dozen times a day:

'Mme Armande said that . . .'

'It was Mme Armande who ordered it . . .'

Later on I began to wonder if she didn't have an ulterior motive in insinuating herself into our house with the excuse of nursing Anne-Marie. It's stupid, I admit.

Over and over again I have reviewed these questions with myself. True, from the purely material point of view, she had spent her mother's inheritance nursing her first husband, and she was now entirely dependent on her father. But the latter enjoyed a very handsome fortune which, at his death, even after being divided among five children, would represent an appreciable amount for each of them.

I also told myself that the old man was erratic, and an autocrat, that people called him 'original' which, with us, means all sorts of thing. She would certainly have wasted her time trying to exercise her power over him and I am convinced that, in the house on the Place Boildieu, she was obliged to play second fiddle.

Is that the key to the problem? I was not wealthy. My profession, as exercised by a man conscious of his limitations like myself, is not one which allows him to pile up a fortune or to live luxuriously.

I am not handsome, your Honour. I went so far as to envisage more audacious hypotheses. My big peasant body, my big face glowing with health, even my ungainliness . . . of course you know that certain women especially among the more emancipated . . .

But it wasn't that either! I know it now. Armande is normally sexed, or rather below normal.

There remains only one explanation. She was living at her father's as she would have lived at a hotel. It was no longer her home.

She entered our house by chance, by accident. And yet . . . Let me explain. I want to get to the bottom of this question, even if it makes you shrug your shoulders. I have told you about her first visit, on the occasion of our first bridge party. I have told you that she saw everything, that she looked at everything with a little smile on her lips.

One tiny incident recurs to me. My mother, showing her the empty drawing-room, said:

'We will probably buy the drawing-room set which was shown last week in Durand-Weil's window.'

Because I had vaguely mentioned it. A drawing-room set done in imitation Beauvais, chairs and settees with gilded legs.

And although we barely knew her, although she had only just entered our house, I saw her nostrils quiver ever so slightly.

I am sorry if I am idiotic, your Honour. But I tell you this: *At that moment Armande knew very well that we would never buy that drawing-room set at Durand-Weil's.* I don't pretend there was any conspiracy. I don't affirm that she knew that she would marry me. I say *know* and I insist upon that word.

Like all peasants I am used to animals. We have had dogs and cats all our life, so intimately mingled with it that when my mother wants to place some recollection, she says for example:

'It was the year we lost our poor Brutus . . .'

Or else:

'It was the time the black cat had kittens under the wardrobe . . .'

And it often happens in the country that an animal starts following you, follows you and no one else, goes into the house with you, and then deliberately and with almost absolute assurance, decides that this house shall, henceforth, be his. In this way, for three years at Bourgneuf, we kept an old yellow half-blind cur, and my father's dogs were forced to put up with him.

He was filthy besides, and I have often heard my father say:

'It would be better to put a bullet through his head ...'

He never did. The animal, whom he had named Jaundice, died peacefully of old age – or, rather, horribly, since it took him three days to die, during which time my mother never stopped applying hot compresses to his belly.

I, too, later on, sometimes thought:

'It would be better to put a bullet through her head.'

And I never did. It was someone else I ...

What I am trying to make you understand, your Honour, is that she came into our house in the most natural way in the world and that, also in the most natural way in the world, she remained.

When it comes to fatalities like this, to inescapable things, it seems as if every one were in a hurry to be fate's accomplice and went out of the way to humour her.

From the very first days my friends fell into the habit of asking me:

'How is Armande?'

And it seemed to them perfectly normal for her to be living in my house, and for them to be coming to me to inquire about her.

After two weeks, during which the disease ran its natural course, people would say with the same artlessness which nevertheless implied so much:

'She is an amazing woman.'

As though, you understand, they considered that she belonged to me already. Even my mother ... I've talked to you enough about Mama for you to know her by this time. To get her son married, that was all very well, since I had not chosen to be a priest . . . But on the express condition that the house should remain hers and that she should continue to run it as she saw fit . . .

Well, your Honour, believe it or not, my mother was the first to say, while after all Armande was in our house only in the capacity of a volunteer nurse, one evening when I expressed surprise at the peas being cooked in a way they had never been before:

'I asked Armande how she liked them. This is the recipe she gave me. Don't you like them?'

Armande called me Charles right away and it was she who asked me to call her by her first name. She was not coquettish. I never saw her, even after we were married, dressed in any but a rather strict way, and I remember a remark I heard about her:

'Mme Alavoine is a statue, if a statue could walk.'

Even after Anne-Marie was well again, she continued to come to the house almost every day. As Mama had very little time to go out with the children, she would call for them and take them for a walk in the gardens of the Prefecture.

My mother used to say to me:

'She is very fond of your daughters.'

One of my patients made a *faux pas*:

'I just ran into your wife and your little girls at the corner of the Rue de la République.'

And Anne-Marie, when we were all together at table one day, said very gravely:

'But, Mama, Armande said so . . .'

By the time we were married six months later, she had already been reigning over the house and the family for a very long time, and it would not have been surprising if the townspeople in speaking of me had said, not:

'That is Dr Alavoine...'

But:

'That is Mme Armande's future husband...'

Have I the right to claim that I did not want to marry her? I acquiesced. First of all there were my two daughters.

'They will be so happy to have a mother...'

Mama was beginning to get old and, refusing to admit it, bustled about from morning to night, wearing herself out at her task.

But no – let's be absolutely sincere. If not, your Honour, what's the use of writing to you at all? I can sum up in two words my state of mind at the time:

First: cowardice.

Second: vanity.

Cowardice because I did not have the courage to say no. Everybody was against me. Everybody by a kind of tacit agreement encouraged the marriage.

But, for this woman who was so amazing, I felt not the least sexual desire. I had felt no particular desire for Jeanne, my first wife, either, but at that time I was young, I married for the sake of being married. In marrying her I did not know that she would leave a large part of me unsatisfied and that all my life I should be tormented by the desire to be unfaithful to her.

With Armande, I knew it. I am going to confess something absurd. Suppose that conventions and wordly wisdom did not exist. I would much rather have married Laurette than the daughter of M. Hilaire de Lanusse.

What's more, I should have preferred our little

servant girl Lucile, with whom I sometimes had intercourse without even giving her time to put down the shoe she happened to be polishing and which she had to keep in her hand, very comically, the whole time.

Only, I was just beginning to practise in the city. I was living in a handsome house. Just the sound of footsteps on the fine gravel of the paths was for me a sign of luxury, and I had finally made myself a present of something I had been coveting, a revolving sprinkler for watering the lawn.

I was not speaking lightly, your Honour, when I told you that one generation, more or less, could be of capital importance.

Armande was I don't know how many generations ahead of me. Her ancestors – we have any number of families like hers in the Vendée – most probably made their fortune buying confiscated property at the time of the Revolution and afterwards ennobled themselves with a *de*.

I am making every effort, you can see that, to get as close to the truth as possible. God knows, at the point I have reached, a little more or a little less doesn't matter. I believe that I am as frank as a man can be. And I am as lucid as one becomes only after one has crossed to the other side.

But that doesn't prevent my being conscious of my impotence. Everything that I have just told you is true and is false. And yet, night after night, stretched out beside Armande in the same bed, I have asked myself the question, I have asked myself why she was there.

And now, your Honour, I ask myself, and this is more serious, if, after having read me, you will not eventually ask yourself the same question, not with regard to my own affairs, but with regard to yours.

I married her.

All right! The same night she slept in my bed. The same night I made love with her, very badly for her and for me. I was embarrassed because I was sweating – I sweat very easily – and because I felt clumsy and inexperienced.

Do you know what was the most difficult thing of all? To kiss her on the mouth. Because of that smile. For, night and day, she keeps an identical smile, which is her natural expression. Well, it isn't easy to kiss a smile like that.

After ten years, I had the impression, whenever I 'climbed her' (as my father would have said), that she was laughing at me.

What haven't I thought on the subject of Armande? You don't know our house. Everybody will tell you that it has become one of the most agreeable houses in La Roche-sur-Yon. Even our old furniture, the few pieces that are left, have taken on such a different aspect that my mother and I hardly recognize them.

Well, for me, it has always been *her house*.

The food is excellent, but it is *her* food.

And my friends? After a year I no longer looked upon them as my friends but *hers*.

And as a matter of fact they all took *her* part later on when things happened – all of them, including the ones I thought my best friends, those I had known as a student, those I had known as a boy.

'You're lucky to have found such a wife!'

Yes, your Honour. Yes, gentlemen. I realize it with due humility. And it is because I realized it, day after day, for ten years that . . .

Forgive me! I'm off the track again. But I have such a strong feeling that it would take a very little effort to get to the bottom of things, once and for all!

In medicine, diagnosis is the thing that counts. Once the malady has been tracked down, it is only a question of routine or the knife. And what I am furiously attempting is a diagnosis.

I never loved Jeanne and I never asked myself if I loved her. I never loved any of the girls I happened to sleep with. I never felt the need, nor the desire. More than that. The word *love*, except in the trivial locution *to make love*, seemed to me a word that a kind of modesty keeps one from pronouncing.

Do people talk about love in the country?

At home they say:

'I went bulling down in the hollow road with the So-and-So girl . . .'

My father really loved my mother, and yet I am sure he never mentioned love. As for Mama, I cannot imagine her pronouncing the sentimental phrases one hears in films or reads in novels.

To Armande I never spoke of love either. One evening when she was dining at the house with my mother and me, we were discussing the colour of the curtains we were going to buy for the dining-room. She favoured red, a very bright red, which terrified Mama.

'You must excuse me,' she said with that smile of hers. 'I am giving my opinion just as if I were at home.'

And I heard myself reply without premeditation, without thinking, as though uttering a banal politeness:

'It only depends on you for it to be so in reality.'

That is how I proposed to her.

'You're joking, Charles.'

My poor Mama seconded me!

'Charles never jokes.'

'You really want me to become Mme Alavoine?'

'In any case' (still my mother at the helm), 'the children will certainly be happy.'

'Who knows? ... Aren't you afraid I'll upset your household too much?'

If Mama had only known! Don't misunderstand me – Armande has always been very sweet to her. She has behaved exactly like a doctor's wife concerned about the comfort, the peace of mind, and the good name of her husband.

Always, without exception and with an innate tact – you must have noticed it yourself in court – she does the right thing.

Wasn't it her first duty to polish my rough edges, since she was more civilized than I and since I, fresh from the country, was trying to make good in the city? Shouldn't she refine my tastes as much as possible, create for my daughters a more delicate atmosphere than the one my mother and I were used to?

All of which she accomplished with a dexterity peculiar to her, and with exquisite tact.

Oh! That word!

'She is exquisite.' For ten years I have had it dinned into my ears in every key. 'You have an exquisite wife.'

And I would come home with an uneasy feeling and such a sensation of my inferiority that I felt like going to eat in the kitchen with the maid.

As for Mama, your Honour, she was made to dress in black or grey silk, made to dress in a dignified and becoming manner. She was made to arrange her hair differently – before that her bun was always straggling down the nape of her neck – and she was made to sit in the drawing-room in front of a charming little work-table with her sewing.

She was forbidden, for the sake of her health, to come downstairs before nine o'clock, and her breakfast was brought to her in bed – Mama who at home used to feed the animals – the cows, the chickens and the pigs – before sitting down to eat herself!

On her birthday and holidays she was presented with tasteful gifts, including old-lady jewellery.

'Don't you think, Charles, that Mama seems a little tired this summer?'

She was urged, but this time in vain, to go to Evian to take the cure for her liver, with which she had had some difficulties.

And all that, your Honour, is perfect. Everything Armande has done, everything she does, everything she will ever do is perfect. Do you realize how discouraging that could be?

On the witness-stand she appeared neither as a heart-broken nor as an irate wife. She did not wear black. She did not call upon society to punish me, nor did she make an appeal for pity. She was simple and calm. She was herself – serene.

It was entirely her idea to engage the services of Maître Gabriel, the most famous leader of the Paris bar (also the most expensive advocate) – her idea also, since I belonged in a way to La Roche-sur-Yon, that it would be a dignified thing to have the Vendée represented by its best lawyer.

She answered all the questions with a naturalness that caused general admiration and several times I really thought that the courtroom was going to burst into applause.

Do you remember the way she said, when my crime was mentioned:

'I have nothing to say concerning this woman ... I received her two or three times at the house, but I hardly knew her ...'

Without hate, as the newspapers were careful to emphasize. Almost without bitterness. And with what dignity!

That's it, your Honour. I think I have just found the right word unwittingly. Armande has *dignity*. She is dignity itself. And now, try to imagine yourself for ten years in daily tête-à-têtes with Dignity, try to picture yourself in the same bed with Dignity!

I shouldn't say that. It is false, utterly false. I know it, but I have only just discovered it. I had to make the great leap first. Yet I really must explain, try to make you understand my former state of mind during the years of my married life.

Have you ever dreamed that you had married your schoolmistress? Well, your Honour, that is what happened to me. For ten years my mother and I, both of us, lived at school, waiting to be given a good mark, in fear of receiving a bad one.

And my mother is still there.

Suppose you are walking along a calm street in a provincial town, on a hot August afternoon. The street is divided in two by the line separating the shady side from the sunny side.

You walk along the pavement flooded with sunlight and your shadow walks along with you almost at your side; you can see it broken in two by the angle formed by the white-walled houses and the pavement.

Go on supposing . . . Do make the effort . . . All at once, this shadow accompanying you disappears . . .

It doesn't change its position. It doesn't pass behind you because you have changed your direction. I mean, it just disappears.

And suddenly there you are in the street without a shadow. You turn round and you can't find it. You look down at your feet and your feet emerge from a pool of sunlight.

The houses on the other side of the street still hold their cool shadows. Chatting peacefully, two men pass by and their shadows precede them, moving in the same cadence, making the same gestures.

There is a dog by the kerb. He, too, has his shadow.

You begin to feel yourself all over. Your body has the same consistency as on any other day. You take a few quick steps and you stop short, hoping to find your shadow again. You run. Still it is not there. You turn on your heel and look down, there is no dark spot on the bright stones of the pavement.

The world is full of reassuring shadows. The shadow of the church on the square alone covers a vast area, where a few old men sit enjoying the cool shade.

You are not dreaming. You have no shadow and, seized with anguish, you stop a passer-by:

'I beg your pardon . . .'

He stops. He looks at you. You do exist then, even if you have lost your shadow. He waits to know what you want of him.

'This is the market-place, isn't it?'

And he thinks you must be crazy, or else a stranger.

Can you imagine the anguish of wandering alone without a shadow in a world where everybody else has one?

I don't know whether I dreamed this or whether I read it somewhere. When I first began to talk to you about it, I thought I was inventing a comparison; then it seemed to me that this anguish of the man without a shadow was somehow familiar, that I had lived it before, that it was bringing back confused memories, and so I believe it may be a forgotten dream.

For years – I don't know just how many – five or six – I went about the city like everybody else. Had anyone asked me if I were happy, I would have absent-mindedly answered yes.

You see that all I have told you before is not really so exact. My house was being organized, became little by little more comfortable and more attractive. My girls were growing up. The elder made her first communion. My clientele increased – not a wealthy clientele, but the common people. That doesn't bring in as much per visit, but the common people pay cash after coming into your office with your fee in their hand.

I learned to play bridge correctly and that occupied me for several months. We bought a car and that took up some more time. I started playing tennis again because Armande played tennis, which accounted for a considerable number of late afternoons.

All this joined together – these little initiations, these hopes for further improvement, this looking forward to trivial pleasures, to minor joys, and banal satisfactions – ended by filling up five or six years of my life.

'Next summer we'll go to the seashore for our vacation.'

Another year there were the winter sports. Another year something else.

As for this business of the shadow, it did not happen all at once, as in the case of my man on the street. But I couldn't find any better image.

I can't even place the thing within a year or so. My disposition apparently did not change, I did not lose my appetite, and I had the same inclination for work.

There just came a moment when I began to look around me with different eyes and I saw a city that looked strange to me, a pretty city, very neat, very luminous, very clean, a city in which everybody greeted me affably.

Why did I have that sensation of emptiness then?

I began looking at my house too, and I asked myself why it was my house, what connexion there was between these rooms, this garden, this wrought-iron gate adorned with a brass plate bearing my name, and me.

I looked at Armande and I had to keep telling myself that she was my wife.

Why?

And these little girls who called me Papa . . .

I repeat, it didn't happen all at once, for, in that case, I would have been very much worried about myself and would have consulted one of my colleagues.

What was I doing in a peaceful little town, in a charming comfortable house among people who smiled at me and cordially shook my hand?

And who had fixed the order of my days, which I followed as scrupulously as if my life depended on it? What am I saying! As if from the beginning of time it had been decided by the Creator that this order should inexorably be mine!

We entertained frequently, twice or three times a

week. Good friends, who had their day, their habits, their little foibles, their armchair. And I watched them with a certain terror, saying:

'What have I to do with them?'

It was as if my sight had grown too keen, as if, for example, it had suddenly become sensitive to ultra-violet rays.

And I was the only one to see the world in this way, the only one to be troubled in a universe that had no idea of what was happening to me.

In fact, for years and years I lived without being conscious of all this. I had scrupulously done the best I could, everything I had been told to do. Without trying to know the reason. Without trying to understand.

A man must have a profession, and Mama had made a doctor of me. He must have children, and I had children. He must have a house, a wife, and I had all these. He must have distractions, and I drove a car, played bridge and tennis. He must have vacations, and I took my family to the seashore.

My family! I would look at them around the dining-room table and it was as if I didn't recognize them. I would look at my daughters. Everybody said they resembled me.

In what way? Why?

And what was this woman doing in my house, in my bed?

And these people sitting patiently in my waiting-room, whom I called into my office, one by one? . . .

Why?

I continued to go through the same daily motions. I was not unhappy, you mustn't think that, but I had the impression of running around in circles.

Then, little by little, a vague longing took possession of me, so vague that I hardly know how to speak of it. I lacked something and I didn't know what. Often my mother, between meals, will say:

'I think maybe I'm a little bit hungry.'

She isn't sure. Just a diffused uneasiness which she quickly satisfies by eating a piece of bread and butter or some cheese.

I too was hungry, undoubtedly, but for what?

It came so insensibly, this uneasiness, that it is impossible, I repeat, to date the beginning of it within a year or two. I paid no attention to it. We have been so conditioned to think that what exists, exists; that the world is really as we see it, that we must do this or that and never act otherwise . . .

I shrugged my shoulders.

'Bah! A slight depression . . .'

Was it, perhaps, because of Armande, who did not give me enough rein?

That is what I decided one day, and thenceforth it was Armande and Armande alone who for me epitomized the over-calm city, the over-harmonious house, the family, work, all that was too monotonous in my daily existence.

'She is the one who wants to keep it like this. She who keeps me from being free, from living the life of a real man.'

I watched her. I spied on her. Every word of hers, every gesture, confirmed me in my idea.

'She's the one who insisted on having the house as it is, on organizing our life in a certain way, on my living as she sees fit . . .'

And that, your Honour, is what I have understood

recently. Armande, little by little, without knowing it herself, took on for me the character of Destiny. And, in revolt against that Destiny, I revolted against her.

'She's so jealous she won't allow me one moment of liberty.'

Was it jealousy? I sometimes wonder. Perhaps simply because she believed that a wife's place was by her husband's side?

About this time I went to Caen, for my aunt had just died. I went alone. I can't remember what kept Armande at home, probably the illness of one of the children, for one or the other of them was almost always ill.

Passing by the little street, I remembered the girl with the red hat, and the blood rushed to my head. I thought I understood what it was I needed. That evening, in my mourning clothes, I went to the Brasserie Chandivert which I found almost unchanged, except for a few additional lights. It seems to me that the place is more spacious now and that they have still further enlarged it at the back.

I was seeking, I wanted the same adventure. With a sort of anguish I looked round at all the women sitting alone. Not one of them resembled even vaguely the girl of the past.

What of it! I felt the need of deceiving Armande, of deceiving my Destiny as sordidly as possible, and I chose a big blonde with a vulgar smile and a gold tooth in the front of her mouth.

'You're a stranger here, aren't you?'

She did not take me home with her, but to a little hotel behind the church of St John. Her gestures in getting undressed were so professional that it sickened me, and at a certain moment I was on the point of leaving.

'How much will you pay me?'

And then suddenly it took possession of me. It was like a need for vengeance, I can't think of any other word. Surprised, she kept repeating, showing her gold tooth:

'Well, I'll be damned! . . .'

That, your Honour, is the first time I was unfaithful to Armande. I put into it as much fury as if I had been trying at any cost to find my shadow.

Chapter Five

The clock outside the station, a great reddish moon suspended in darkness, showed six minutes to seven. Just as I opened the door of my taxi, the big hand advanced one minute, and I remember clearly its jerky movement and how it went on quivering as though, having started too impetuously, it could with difficulty contain itself. A train whistled – mine probably. I was encumbered with a lot of little packages which were threatening to come undone; the taxi-driver could not change the note I handed him. It was pouring and, with my feet in a puddle of water, I had to unbutton my overcoat and my jacket and search through my pockets for small change.

Another taxi drew up in front of mine. A young woman got out, looked round in vain for a porter – there is never one to be had when it is raining – and finally, carrying her two heavy-looking suitcases herself, made a dash for the station.

We were to meet again a few moments later, one behind the other, in front of the ticket window.

'La Roche-sur-Yon, second class, single . . .'

Taller than she, I could see, by looking over her shoulder, the inside of her handbag lined with moiré silk – a handkerchief, a compact, a cigarette lighter, letters, and keys. I had only to repeat what she had just said:

'La Roche-sur-Yon, second class, single.'

I gathered up all my little packages. I ran. A station attendant opened a glass door, and when I reached the platform the train was just pulling out; with my ridiculous cargo it was impossible for me to jump on to the step of the moving train. One of my friends, Deltour, the garage owner, standing in the doorway of one of the compartments, waved to me. It is unbelievable how long it takes a train you have just missed to leave. The cars seem to continue to move interminably along the platform.

As I turned I noticed, standing close beside me, the young woman of the two suitcases.

'We've missed it,' she said.

In fact, your Honour, those were the very first words Martine said to me. They strike me for the first time as I write them.

'We've missed it . . .'

Don't you find that extraordinary?

I wasn't too sure that she was addressing me. She did not seem too much put out.

'Do you know what time there's another train?'

'At ten twelve . . .'

And I looked at my watch, which was idiotic since there was an enormous luminous clock facing the platform.

'Well, the only thing to do in the meantime is to put

our baggage in the cloakroom,' she said, and again I couldn't be sure whether she was talking to herself or trying to start a conversation.

Although the platform was covered, large drops were leaking through the glass roof on to the rails. A station is like a tunnel; except that, contrary to tunnels, the interior is light and the darkness at both ends, with a chill wind blowing towards you.

Mechanically I followed her. She had not actually suggested it. Being sufficiently loaded down myself, I could not help her with her bags, and it was I who had to stop twice to pick up the packages I appeared to be juggling.

Alone, I would not have thought of the cloakroom. It never occurs to me. I am more inclined to pile up my things beside me in some familiar café or restaurant. I should undoubtedly have had dinner at the buffet in the station and read the papers in my corner until time for the next train.

'You live at La Roche-sur-Yon?'

I said yes.

'Do you know M. Boquet?'

'Of the Galleries?'

'Yes. He is the proprietor of a department store.'

'I know him.'

She opened her bag again, took out a cigarette and lighted it. I was struck by the way she held her cigarette, I can't tell you why. She had a way all her own of holding a cigarette. She gave a little shiver.

It was December, your Honour. A little less than a year ago. One week before Christmas, which explains all my little packages.

I had gone to Nantes with one of my patients who

required an emergency operation. I had made the trip in the ambulance, and that is why I was without my car. Gaillard, the surgeon, had taken me home with him when we left the hospital and given me some raspberry brandy which had been sent to him from Alsace by one of his former patients.

'You are dining with us this evening. But of course you are. My wife is out and if she comes home and doesn't find you here she will be furious with me for having let you go.'

I explained that I absolutely had to catch the six-fifty train, that I had two patients coming the same evening, and that Armande had given me a whole list of things to buy.

That was fatal. I spent two good hours running round the shops. I lost I don't know how much time matching buttons she could probably have found just as well at La Roche. I bought a few toys and other little things for the children. It had been raining all day, and each time I went from one shop to another I would pass through a curtain of driving rain.

Now I found myself in the station beside a young woman I didn't know, and whom I had barely even looked at. We were the only persons at the baggage counter in the middle of a vast empty space. The attendant thought we were together. If it hadn't been for that enveloping space, which gave us a false air of solidarity, I should probably have walked away with as much nonchalance as I could muster.

I didn't quite dare. I noticed that she was cold, that she was wearing a dark tailored suit, very chic, but much too light for the season. She had on a curious little hat, a sort of flower made of satin which she wore over one eye.

She looked pale under her make-up. She shivered again and said:

'I'm going to get something to drink to warm me up . . .'

'At the buffet?'

'No. You can't get anything decent at a buffet. I think I saw an American bar not far from here . . .'

'You don't know Nantes?'

'I arrived this morning . . .'

'Are you going to stay long at La Roche?'

'Perhaps for years, perhaps for ever. That will depend on your friend M. Boquet.'

We were walking towards one of the doors, which I now held open for her.

'If you will allow me . . .'

She did not bother to reply. Quite naturally we crossed the square together in the downpour, avoiding cars, hunching our shoulders, hastening our steps.

'Wait a minute; I arrived from this direction, didn't I? . . . Then it's on the left . . . near the corner of a street . . . There's a big sign in green lights . . .'

I could have gone back to the Gaillards for dinner, or to a dozen other friends who complained every time I came through Nantes without stopping to see them. I was not familiar with the bar she took me to, which was new: a narrow room, dimly lighted, with dark woodwork and high stools in front of the bar. It was the kind of place which did not yet exist in the provinces when I was a student, and I have never quite got used to them.

'Barman, a martini, please . . .'

I'd much rather not talk about her as I saw her that evening, your Honour, but then you wouldn't understand, and my letter would be useless. It is difficult, I assure you, especially now.

Isn't it true, Martine, that it is difficult?

Because, you see, she was such a banal little thing. She was already perched on one of the stools, and one felt that she was at home there, that it was an old habit, that together with the more or less luxurious setting it formed a part of her conception of life.

The cigarette too. She had hardly finished the first one when she lighted another, once more staining it with her lipstick, and turned to the barman, half closing her eyes because of the smoke (I have always hated women who made faces when they smoked).

'Not too much gin for me . . .'

She asked for olives. She munched a clove. She had hardly closed her bag when she opened it again to take out her compact and lipstick.

I was irritated and resigned at the same time. Here's something else that will help you to understand. I love big dogs that are strong and conscious, quietly conscious, of their strength. I have a horror of those little dogs that are never still, that run around after their own tails and insist on attention all the time. Well, that evening she made me think of one of those little dogs.

She lived to be looked at. She must have thought herself very attractive. She did think so. I almost forgot that she herself told me so a little later.

'Is your friend Boquet the kind of man who sleeps with his secretary? I only met him once, by chance, and I didn't have time to ask him . . .'

I don't know what I answered. It was so stupid! Besides, she never waited for an answer. It was only what she said that interested her.

'I wonder what makes every man run after me. It isn't because I'm beautiful, because I'm not. It must be some kind of charm . . .'

A charm which in any case did not work with me. Our glasses were empty, and I must have ordered fresh drinks unless the barman served us of his own accord.

She was thin, and I don't like thin women. She was very dark, and I have a preference for blondes. And she looked like a cover girl.

'Is La Roche nice?'

You see the kind of question.

'Is it boring?'

'Possibly . . .'

There were a few customers, not many, all habitués, as is always the case in places of that sort. And I have noticed that, in no matter what city, they are always the same physical type, dress alike and make use of the same vocabulary.

She looked at them, one after the other, and you felt that she could not live without being noticed.

'No really – he's getting on my nerves, that old codger.'

'Which one?'

'Over there in the left-hand corner. The one in that very light sport suit. In the first place, when you're his age you don't wear a pale green suit! Especially at this time of day and at this season of the year! For the last ten minutes he hasn't stopped smirking at me. If he continues I shall go over and ask him what he wants . . .'

Then a few moments later:

'Let's go! Or I'll slap his face.'

We went out and it was still raining. Like the evening

of the little red hat in Caen. But at the moment, I never once thought of Caen.

'Perhaps we'd better go and have dinner,' she said.

A taxi was passing. I hailed it and we found ourselves together in the damp darkness of the back seat. It occurred to me that it was the first time I had been in a taxi with a strange woman. I could see indistinctly the milky blur of her face, the red light of her cigarette, and two slim silk-stockinged legs. I could smell the odour of her cigarette, of her clothes, and of her wet hair.

If I felt anything – and it was very vague – it was that odour of wet hair.

'I don't know whether we'll find a table at Francis's at this hour, but that's where we're likely to get the best food.'

One of the best restaurants in France! There are three floors of quiet little dining-rooms without any useless luxury, where the maîtres d'hôtels and the wine stewards all look like ancestors, having been with the restaurant since it first opened.

We got a table on the mezzanine, near a half-moon window from which we looked down on the umbrellas passing at our feet. A rather curious effect, in fact.

'A bottle of muscadet to begin with, Doctor?' Joseph, who had known me for a long time, suggested.

And she:

'So you're a doctor . . .'

You don't go to Francis's to stuff yourself but to enjoy good food. With *chevreuil aux morilles*, an old burgundy was indicated. After dinner we were served a special cognac in brandy glasses. She talked all the time, she talked about herself, about the people she knew and who, as though by chance, were all important persons.

'When I was in Geneva . . .'

'Last year at the Negresco, in Nice . . .'

I knew her first name, Martine. I also knew that she had met Raoul Boquet by chance in some bar in Paris – Raoul is a pillar of bars – and that at one o'clock in the morning he had engaged her as his secretary.

'The idea of living in a little provincial city intrigued me . . . Do you believe that? . . . Can you understand that? . . . As for your friend, I warned him that I would not go to bed with him . . .'

At three o'clock that morning, your Honour, I was the one who was in bed with her, loving her furiously, so furiously that she could not help at times giving me a surreptitious glance, in which there was not only curiosity and amazement but real terror as well.

I don't know what came over me. Never had I worked myself into such a frenzy before.

You have just seen how stupid our meeting was. And what happened after that was even stupider.

There was a moment, perhaps several, when I must certainly have been drunk. For example, I have only a blurred recollection of leaving Chez Francis. Before then, with the excuse that it was there I had celebrated my doctor's degree, I insisted – talking much too loudly and gesticulating – that old Francis should come in person to drink with us. Then I seized upon one of the chairs like all the other chairs in the house and swore that I recognized it as the very chair I had sat upon that famous evening.

'I tell you this is the one, and I can prove it – that nick there on the second rung . . . Gaillard was there . . . Gaillard, that jerk! . . . He'll be angry with me for not dining at his house tonight . . . You won't tell him I was here, will you, Francis? ... Word of honour? ...'

We walked. It was I who insisted on strolling in the rain. The streets were almost empty, with puddles of water, puddles of light, and enormous drops falling from the cornices and balconies.

She had some difficulty walking because of her high heels and clung to my arm; from time to time she would have to stop to put on her shoe, which kept coming off.

'I don't know if it still exists, but there used to be a little bistro in this neighbourhood, run by an enormously fat woman ... It isn't far from here ...'

Obstinately, I persisted in trying to find it. We kept on paddling through the wet. And when finally, with our shoulders dripping with rain, we entered a little café which was perhaps the one I was looking for and perhaps not, the clock over the bar said a quarter past ten.

'Is your clock right?'

'It's five minutes slow.'

Then we looked at each other and after a second we both burst out laughing.

'What are you going to say to Armande?'

I must have been talking about Armande. I don't know exactly what I could have said, but I have a vague idea that I tried to be witty at her expense.

In fact, it was in this little café, where there wasn't another soul, where a cat was curled up on a chair near a big iron stove – it was in this café, as I say, that I first realized that we were saying *tu* to each other.

She announced as though it were a choice entertainment:

'We must telephone Armande ... Have you a telephone, Madame?'

'In the hall, to the left . . .'

A narrow hall with walls painted a sickly green led to the lavatories and was impregnated with their smell. The telephone was attached to the wall. There were two receivers, and Martine took possession of one of them. We were touching each other, or at least our wet clothes were touching, and our breath smelled of the calvados we had just drunk at the bar.

'Hello, give me 12-51, please . . . Will I have to wait long? . . .'

We were told to stay on the wire. I don't know why we were laughing, but I remember that I was obliged to hold my hand over the mouthpiece. We heard the operators calling each other.

'Give me 12-51, dear . . . Is it raining as hard there as it is here? . . . What time are you through? . . . Hello! . . . Is this 12-51? . . . One moment . . . Nantes calling . . . Hello, Nantes . . . go ahead . . .'

And all this amused us, God knows why – it all seemed excruciatingly funny.

'Hello . . . Is that you, Armande?'

'Charles? . . . Are you still in Nantes?'

Martine poked me with her elbow.

'I've been detained – there were complications. I had to go back to the hospital to see my patient . . .'

'Did you have dinner with the Gaillards?'

'That is . . .'

Martine was leaning against me. I was afraid she was going to burst out laughing again. I wasn't very proud of myself, as you may imagine . . .

'No . . . I didn't want to bother them . . . I had shopping to do . . .'

'Did you find my buttons?'

'Yes . . . and the toys for the children . . .'

'Are you at the Gaillards' now?'

'No . . . I'm still in town . . . I've just left the hospital . . .'

'Will you spend the night with them?'

'I wonder . . . I'd almost rather go to the hotel . . . I am tired and with Gaillard it will mean staying up till one o'clock in the morning again . . .'

Silence. All this seemed odd to my wife. I swallowed hard when she asked:

'You're alone?'

'Yes . . .'

'You're telephoning from a café?'

'I'm going to a hotel . . .'

'To the Duc de Bretagne?'

'Probably. If they have a room.'

'What have you done with the packages?'

'I have them here with me . . .'

'Well, don't lose them . . . By the way, Mme Gringuois came this evening . . . She said she had an appointment for nine o'clock . . . She still has pain and insisted on waiting . . .'

'I'll see her tomorrow morning.'

'You'll take the first train?'

What else could I do? The six thirty-two, in the dark, in the cold, in the rain! And very often, as I knew, the carriages weren't heated.

'Until tomorrow . . .'

I repeated:

'Until tomorrow . . .'

I had hardly hung up when Martine exclaimed:

'She didn't believe you . . . It was what you said about the packages she didn't swallow . . .'

We drank another calvados at the bar and plunged once more into the wet darkness of the streets. We were in the gay stage of intoxication. Everything made us laugh. We made fun of the few people we passed in the street. We made fun of Armande, of my patient, Mme Gringuois, whom I must have told her about.

Music coming from behind a façade brightly illuminated with neon lights attracted us, and we found ourselves in a little night club, narrow and red all over. The lights were red, red the velvet covering of the benches, red the walls on which nude figures were painted, red the soiled dinner-jackets of the five musicians who made up the orchestra.

Martine wanted to dance and I danced with her. That was when I noticed the nape of her neck, very close and very white, with skin so fine that the blue veins showed, and little tendrils of wet hair.

Why did her neck move me? It was, in a way, the first human thing I discovered about her. It had nothing to do with a magazine cover, with a young woman who thought herself very smart. It was the nape of a sickly girl and, as I danced, I began brushing it with my lips.

When we sat down at our table again, I looked at her face with different eyes. She had dark circles under her eyes. The lipstick no longer covered her lips evenly. She was tired, but refused to give in. She wanted, at any cost, to enjoy herself.

'Ask them if they have any whisky . . .'

We began drinking whisky. Somewhat unsteadily she went over to the musicians to ask for some song I didn't know, and I could see her gesticulating.

Another time, she left to go to the Ladies' Room. She

was gone a long time. I wondered if she were sick. I didn't like to go to find out.

I realized now that she was simply a woman and nothing else, a girl, about twenty-five probably, who was bent on showing off. It was at least a quarter of an hour before she returned. For a second time, as she came into the room, I saw her face in repose and it was tired and lined; then immediately she began to smile again. She had hardly sat down when she lighted a cigarette and emptied her glass, but not without a slight retch which she tried to cover up.

'Feel sick?'

'I'm better ... It's all right now ... I'm not used to dinners like that any more ... Won't you order something to drink?'

She was nervous, on edge.

'These last few weeks in Paris have been difficult ... I quit my job, stupidly ...'

She had got rid of her dinner. And now she was drinking again. She wanted to dance. And, as she danced, her body kept pressing against mine.

There was something sad, something forced, about her excitation which somehow moved me. Little by little, I could feel desire growing in me, and it was a kind of desire I had never met before.

You see, your Honour, she was exciting herself. Do you understand?

It wasn't I, it wasn't even the male that counted. I understood later. But, at the moment, I was troubled and baffled. Her desire, in spite of my presence, was a solitary desire.

And her sexual excitement was a laboured excitement. She clung to it as though to escape a void.

At the same time, paradoxical though it may seem, it mortified her, made her suffer.

Once, I remember, just after we had returned to our table and the orchestra was playing the haunting music she had asked for, she suddenly dug her nails into my thigh.

We had drunk a great deal, I don't know how many drinks. We were finally the only customers left in the place and the staff were waiting for us to go so that they could close up. In the end they politely put us out.

It was after two o'clock in the morning. I didn't like to take her to the Duc de Bretagne, where I was known and where I had stayed with Armande and the children.

'Are you sure there's no other place open?'

'Nothing but a few little dumps round the harbour.'

'Let's go . . .'

We took a taxi which we were a long time finding at that hour. And this time, in the darkness of the taxi, brusquely she glued her lips to mine in a kind of spasm, without tenderness, without love. She did not repulse my hand which was on her hip, and I could feel her body so thin, so burning hot, through her wet garments.

What happened was what always happens in such cases. Most of the places were closed or closing as we arrived. We went into a cheap dance hall, and I saw Martine's nostrils quiver because all the men stared at her and she probably sensed danger.

'You want to dance?'

She challenged them with her glance, with her half-open mouth, pressing her thigh harder and harder against mine as she imagined their lust for her.

We were served some horrible brandy that nauseated

us. I was anxious to leave. But I was afraid to insist too much, because I knew what she would think.

In the end we went to a second-class hotel, or more exactly, a fairly good hotel, banally dull, where there was still a light showing and where the night porter, fumbling with the keys hanging on a board, murmured:

'A room with two beds?'

She said nothing. Nor did I. I simply asked to be called at quarter to six. I had no baggage. Martine's suitcases were still in the baggage room at the station and we had not bothered to go for them.

As soon as the door closed, she said:

'We'll each sleep in our own bed, won't we?'

I promised. I was firmly decided on that. There was a tiny bathroom and she went in at once, admonishing me:

'You go on to bed . . .' We were saying *vous* again.

Hearing her moving about, opening and closing the taps, suddenly, your Honour, I had a strange sensation of intimacy. A sensation of intimacy, believe it or not, that I have never had with Armande.

I wonder if I was still drunk. I don't think so. I got undressed and slid under the covers. As she seemed to be taking a long time and I thought she might be sick again, I called out:

'Are you all right?'

'Yes,' she replied. 'Are you in bed?'

'Yes . . .'

'I'm coming . . .'

I had discreetly turned out the light in the room, so that when she opened the bathroom door she was lighted only from behind.

She seemed to me smaller and even thinner. She was

naked and was holding a towel up in front of her, without, I must admit, the least ostentation, even with genuine simplicity.

She turned to switch off the light in the bathroom and I saw her naked back with each vertebra sticking out and her tiny waist, but hips much larger than I had imagined. It was only a matter of seconds. But that image has never left me. I thought something to this effect:

'A poor little girl . . .'

I heard her groping in the dark for her bed. She murmured gently:

'Good night . . .'

Then remarked:

'It's true we haven't much time to sleep. What time is it now?'

'I don't know . . . Wait, I'll turn on the light . . .'

I had only to stretch out my bare arm. My watch was on the bedside table.

'Half-past three . . .'

I saw her hair spread out against the stark whiteness of the pillow. I saw the outline of her body lying with her knees curled up. I even noticed, in spite of the covers, that, like so many little girls, she slept with her hands clasped between the intimate warmth of her thighs. I repeated:

'Good night . . .'

'Good night . . .'

I turned out the light, and yet we did not sleep. Two or three times within a quarter of an hour she turned over in her bed with a sigh.

I swear, your Honour, there was nothing premeditated about it. At one moment I even thought I was falling asleep, I began to feel drowsy.

And it was then that, suddenly, I leaped out of bed and crossed over to hers. My face, my lips, sought her dark hair and I stammered:

'Martine . . .'

Perhaps her first reaction was to push me away! We could not see each other. We were blind, both of us.

I threw back the covers. As in a dream, without pausing, without thinking, hardly knowing what I was doing, with an irresistible movement and without warning, I penetrated her.

At the same instant, I had the sensation of a revelation. It seemed to me that for the first time in my life I possessed a woman.

I loved her furiously. I have told you that. I loved her entire body, feeling its slightest tremors. Our mouths became one, and in a kind of rage I tried to assimilate this flesh which, only a short time before, had meant nothing to me.

Once more, as at the night club of the red lights, I felt those tremors of her body, only more violent now. I almost shared her mysterious anguish, which I was trying to understand.

If we were alone together, your Honour, I would like to give you a few details, only to you, and I should not consider it a profanation. In a letter, I would seem to be taking pleasure in evoking more or less erotic images.

How far I am from all that! Have you ever had the sensation that you were on the point of attaining something superhuman?

That sensation – I tell you, I had it that night. It seemed that I could, if I tried, pierce I know not what ceiling, leap suddenly into unknown regions of space.

And that anguish growing in her . . . that anguish

which, even as a doctor, I could only explain as a desire similar to mine . . .

I am a prudent man, what people call an honest man. I have a wife and children. If sometimes I sought love or pleasure away from home, I had never until that moment risked anything that might, in any way, complicate my family life. You do understand me, don't you?

But with this woman, whom I didn't even know a few hours before, I behaved, in spite of myself, in every respect like a consummate lover – like an animal.

Suddenly, because I didn't understand, my hand groped for the electric switch. I saw her in the yellow glare and I don't know if she realized that from then on her face was in the light.

Throughout her entire being, your Honour, in her staring eyes, in her open mouth, in her pinched nostrils, there was an intolerable anguish, but at the same time – try to understand – a will, no less desperate, to escape, to burst the bubble, to pierce the ceiling – in a word, to be delivered.

I saw this anguish growing towards such a paroxysm that my doctor's conscience took fright, and I felt relieved when suddenly after a final tension of every nerve, she fell back as though empty and discouraged, with her heart throbbing so hard under her little breast that I had no need of touching her to count the beats.

I did so nevertheless, a doctor's obsession. Fear perhaps of the responsibility? Her pulse was a hundred and forty, her colourless lips were parted over her white teeth, as white as the teeth of a corpse.

She murmured something that sounded like:

'I can't . . .'

And she tried to smile. She seized my great paw. She clung to it.

We remained like that for a long time in the stillness of the hotel, waiting for the pulsations to become more normal.

'Get me a glass of water, *veux-tu?*'

She didn't think of pulling the covers over her and you don't know how grateful I am to her for that. While I was holding up her head for her to drink, I noticed a scar, still fresh, on her belly, an angry pick scar running vertically.

You see, for me, a doctor, the scar was rather what an extract from a criminal record would be for you.

She made no attempt to hide it from me. She half stammered:

'Oh God, but I'm tired . . .'

And two great hot tears rolled down my cheeks.

Chapter Six

Are those things that I have told in court, that I could have told you in the silence of your office, in the presence of your redheaded clerk and of Maître Gabriel, for whom life is so simple?

I don't know whether my love for her began that night, but what I am certain of is that when a little before seven o'clock next morning we took a train, clammy with dampness and cold, I could no longer face the prospect of life without her, and that this woman sitting opposite me, pale and blurred in the cruel light of the compartment, near the window on which the raindrops showed lighter than the night – that this stranger, with a hat rendered ridiculous by yesterday's rain, was closer to me than any human being had ever been before.

It would be difficult to be emptier than we were then, both of us, and we must have seemed like phantoms to people who saw us. When the night porter, the same one who had given us our key, came to wake us, a light still shone under the door, for our bedlight had not been turned off since I had gropingly switched it on. Martine was in her bath. I opened the door, wearing only my trousers, with my chest bare and hair tousled, to ask:

'Could you get us some coffee?'

The porter too looked like a phantom.

'I'm sorry, sir, not before seven o'clock.'

'Could you make some for us yourself?'

'I haven't the keys, I'm sorry.'

Was he perhaps a little afraid of me? Outside we couldn't find a taxi. Martine clung to my arm and I probably looked just as spectral in the cold grey mist. And it was lucky for us that our nocturnal peregrinations had landed us not too far from the station.

'Perhaps the buffet will be open.'

It was. Early morning customers were served black coffee or coffee with hot milk in great ashy-white bowls. Just to look at those bowls made my stomach turn over. Martine had insisted on drinking hers and an instant later, without having time to run to the lavatories, lost it right there on the platform.

We did not talk. We sat waiting apprehensively for the effect of the jolting of the train on our aching temples, on all our ailing flesh. Like many morning trains on branch lines, ours kept executing all sorts of manoeuvres before starting, each time hammering our poor heads with violent blows.

Yet she managed to look at me with a smile as we crossed the bridge over the Loire. My little packages were scattered on the seat beside me. We were alone in the compartment. I was still holding my pipe in my mouth, probably with an air of disgust, for I'd had to let it go out.

She murmured:

'I wonder what Armande will say . . .'

I was hardly shocked. A little bit, just the same. But, after all, hadn't I been the one to start it?

'And you? Is any one expecting you?'

'M. Boquet promised to find me a furnished apartment where I could cook . . .'

'Did you sleep with him?'

It was appalling, your Honour. It hadn't been twelve hours since I'd met her. The same reddish-faced clock that had witnessed our meeting was still there behind us, overlooking a network of tracks, and its little hand had not yet completed its course round the dial. And I knew, by her scar, not only that this seedy-looking young woman had had lovers but that she had been shamefully marked.

In spite of that, as I asked the question, suddenly there was a frightful pain in my chest. I remained as though petrified. I had never known anything like it before, but after that, it happened often enough for me to feel a fraternal sympathy for all cardiac sufferers.

'I told you I didn't even have time to speak to him about that . . .'

I had taken it for granted at one time that once in the

train on neutral ground, we would resume the formal *vous*, together with our normal personalities, but, to my astonishment, the *tu* continued to seem perfectly natural.

'If you knew how funny it was the way we met . . .'

'Was he drunk?'

If I asked that right away, it was because I knew Raoul Boquet so well. I have described the American bar at Nantes. We have recently acquired one like it at La Roche-sur-Yon. I haven't set foot in it more than once or twice. You'll find mostly snobs there, who think the city's cafés not smart enough and who go there to show off, perching on the high stools and watching the cocktails being mixed, just the way Martine did the day before. You'll see a few women too, not prostitutes but more probably respectable housewives who want to appear modern. Boquet is something else again. He is my age, perhaps a year or two younger. His father was the founder of the Galleries and he, together with his brother and sister, inherited it five years ago.

Raoul Boquet drinks for the sake of drinking, is rude for the sake of being rude because everything, as he says, is such a goddamn bore – everything and everybody bores him. Because his wife is a goddamn bore he sometimes stays away for four or five days at a time. He will leave the house to be gone an hour, without an overcoat, and turn up two days later in La Rochelle or Bordeaux with a whole bunch of people he has picked up God knows where.

Business too is a goddamn bore, except in spurts, at which times, almost sober for two or three weeks, he begins to turn everything topsy-turvy in the store.

He drives like a madman. On purpose. After midnight

he will suddenly dash up on the pavement for the pleasure of scaring the wits out of some worthy citizen on his way home. He's had I don't know how many accidents. They've taken his licence away twice.

I knew him better than anyone else did, since he was my patient, and suddenly he entered my life in an entirely new capacity, and I was even reduced to being afraid of him.

'He drinks a lot, doesn't he? I thought right away that that interests him more than women . . .'

Except women in certain houses where he goes periodically and raises hell.

'I was with a girl I knew at a bar in Paris, Rue Washington . . . Perhaps you know it? . . . On the left, near the Champs-Elysées. He had been drinking and talked in a loud voice to the man next to him, a friend perhaps, perhaps a stranger . . .'

Her words flowed on monotonously, like the raindrops trickling down the train windows.

' "I'll tell you something," he was saying, "my brother-in-law gives me a pain in the neck. He's a snake, my brother-in-law, but the trouble is, he must be good because my bitch of a sister can't get along without him, swears by him . . . Only the day before yesterday he took advantage of my absence to sack my secretary on some pretext or other . . . The minute he sees a secretary's devoted to me, he sacks her or manages to win her over to his side – easy enough since they all come from around there . . .

' "I ask you, do the Galleries belong to the Boquets or don't they? And is he a Boquet when he's called Machoul? I'm telling you, barman, Machoul, that's his name, if you have no objection . . . My brother-in-law's name is Machoul, and the only thing he thinks about is how he can kick me out too . . .

' "And do you know what I'm going to do, old man? I'm going to get my next secretary from Paris, a girl who doesn't know Oscar Machoul and who won't be impressed by him." '

The sky was beginning to get lighter. Silhouetted against the uniform greyness of the flat countryside, farms began to come out of the shadows, with lights in the stables.

Martine went on talking, without hurrying.

'I had come to the end of my tether, you know. I was drinking cocktails with my friend because she was paying for them, but for eight days I'd been living on nothing but rolls and coffee. All at once, I went over to him, and I said:

'If you want a secretary who doesn't know Machoul, take me . . .'

I understood a lot of things, your Honour, I can tell you. And first of all, knowing Boquet as I do, I could picture the scene. He must have talked as crudely as possible, on principle.

'You're broke, I suppose.'

And he undoubtedly asked her with a false air of innocence if she'd been working in an office or *en maison*.

'Well, come along to La Roche if you like, we can always try it.'

He made her drink, that is certain. One of the reasons I always keep away from the bar where he hangs out is that he gets furious if anyone has the misfortune to refuse to drink with him.

Anyhow, she came to La Roche, your Honour. She

started out, with her two suitcases, for a little city entirely unknown to her.

'Why did you come by way of Nantes and why did you break your journey there?'

'Because I knew a girl who works at the Belgian Consulate, a friend of mine. I had just enough money left to pay for my railway ticket and I didn't want to ask my new boss for money the minute I arrived.'

Our train stopped at every little station along the line. Each time the brakes were put on we would both give a little start at the same time and then wait in anguish for more jolts as the train moved again. The windows grew pale. Men shouted the names of the stations, rushed up and down, opened and closed the train doors, piled up the mail bags and express packages on hand-carts.

A funny atmosphere, your Honour, in which to say shamefacedly, after hesitating for I don't know how many kilometres:

'You're not going to sleep with him?'

'Of course not.'

'Even if he asks you to? Even if he insists?'

'Of course not.'

'Not with him or anyone else?'

Again that agonizing pain which my patients who suffer from angina pectoris have so often tried to describe to me. You think you are dying. You feel death at hand. You are as though suspended to life by a thread. And yet, I do not have angina pectoris.

'Not with him or anybody else?'

'I promise,' she replied, smiling at me.

We had not mentioned love. We did not mention it then. We were two miserable bedraggled dogs in the unrelieved greyness of that second-class compartment in December, while the day, for want of sun, was slow in rising.

Yet, I believed her, and she believed me.

We were not sitting on the same bench, but opposite each other, for we had to be very careful of our movements to avoid being sick and, at each jolt of the train, bells clanged inside our skulls.

We looked at each other as if we had known each other all our lives. Without coquetry, thank God. It was only shortly before we reached La Roche when she saw me gather my packages together, that she began powdering and putting on lipstick; then she tried lighting a cigarette.

It wasn't on my account, your Honour. For me, she knew that all that was unnecessary. For other people? I wonder. Out of habit, more likely. Or rather, so as not to feel so naked, for we both of us felt almost as naked as in our hotel room.

'Listen, Martine. It is too early to telephone Boquet and the Galleries don't open until nine. I'll leave you at the Hotel de l'Europe. It would be better for you to sleep for a few hours.'

It was evident that she wanted to ask a question and had been hesitating about it for some time and I, I don't know why – I wanted to avoid it, I was afraid of it. She looked at me, resigned and *obedient* – you hear that, obedient – and she simply said:

'Very well.'

'I'll telephone you before noon, or I'll come to see you ... Wait ... no ... I can't come because I have office hours then .. You come to see me ... Anyone can come to a doctor's office ...'

'But Armande?'

'Just come straight to the waiting-room like any patient . . .'

Ridiculous, isn't it? But I was so afraid of losing her! I didn't want her to see Boquet, no matter what happened. I was already unwilling for her to see anyone. I didn't yet know it myself. On the back of an old envelope I drew a plan of part of the city, showing her how to get from the hotel to my house.

At the station I hailed a porter I knew, and I was suddenly very proud of being known.

'Find us a taxi, Prosper, will you?'

I walked behind her, I walked in front of her. I trotted all round her like a shepherd dog. And for a few minutes, I swear, I even forgot my hangover.

In the taxi, although the driver knew me, I held Martine's hand, I was leaning over her like a man in love, and I was not ashamed.

'Above all, don't go out, don't telephone anyone until you've seen me . . . It is eight o'clock . . . Say you sleep until eleven, or even eleven thirty . . . Wednesdays, my office hours are until one o'clock . . . You must promise that you won't see anyone, that you won't telephone anyone . . . Promise me, Martine . . .'

I wonder if she was aware that something extraordinary was happening to her.

'I promise.'

We didn't kiss each other. The Place Napoleon was empty when the taxi stopped in front of the Hotel de l'Europe. I went to find Angèle, the owner, in the kitchen where she was giving the chef orders for the day.

'I want a nice room for a young woman who is very tired and who has been recommended to me by one of my Paris colleagues.'

'Certainly, Doctor . . .'

I did not go up with her. When I had gone down a couple of steps towards the street I turned to look back. Through the glass of the front door, its brasses dulled by the dampness, I saw her standing on the red carpet of the hall talking to Angèle and pointing out her two suitcases to the bell-boy. I saw her, but she did not see me. She was speaking, and I did not hear her voice. For a second, not more, I imagined her mouth open, as I had seen it, you know, the night before, and the idea of leaving her even for such a short time was so intolerable – fear struck me so forcibly – that I almost went back to take her along with me.

When I was alone in the taxi, all my fatigue and all my aches returned – the shooting pains in my temples and that racking sensation in my chest.

'Shall I take you home, Doctor?'

Home, yes. Of course. *Home.* And the seat was piled with little packages, including the famous buttons for a jacket Armande was having made from her own design by the best dressmaker in La Roche-sur-Yon.

Home, since this man said so! Besides there was my name on the brass plate attached to the gate. Babette, our latest maid, came running out to take my packages from the driver, and a curtain stirred on the second floor in my daughters' room.

'You're not too tired, sir? I hope you'll have some breakfast first. Mme Alavoine has already sent down twice to ask if you were back. That train was late again, wasn't it? That's just what I told her!'

The hall with its creamy white walls and, on the hat-rack, coats of mine, my hats, my cane. The voice of my youngest child upstairs:

'Is that you, Papa? Did you see Santa Claus?'

I asked Babette:

'Are there many patients already?'

Because at poor people's doctors patients have to wait their turn and come early. The smell of coffee. That morning it nauseated me. I took off my wet shoes and there was a large hole in one of my socks.

'Why, your feet are soaking, sir!'

'Hush, Babette . . .'

I went up the white staircase with its rose-red carpet held in place by brass rods. I kissed my oldest daughter who was leaving for school. Armande was supervising the other little girl's bath.

'I still don't understand why you didn't spend the night at Gaillard's as usual . . . When you telephoned me last night you didn't seem quite yourself . . . You're not ill, are you? . . . Has anything upset you?'

'No, everything's all right . . . I did all the shopping.'

'I'll look at the things when I come downstairs . . . Mme Gringuois telephoned again this morning and insisted that you go to see her the moment you get back . . . She can't come to the office . . . She waited for two hours last night in the drawing-room, entertaining me with all her troubles . . .'

'I'll change and go right away.'

At the door I turned, like a dolt.

'By the way . . .'

'What?'

'Nothing . . . I'll see you later . . .'

I had been on the point of blurting out that someone was coming for luncheon, someone I had met by chance, the daughter of a friend, I don't know what, I was ready to invent anything at all. It was childish, clumsy. But I had just decided that Martine was going to lunch at the house. I felt that she must take her first meal at La Roche in the intimacy of my home and even, you may think what you like of me, that she must meet Armande, about whom I had talked so much.

I took my bath, I shaved, I got my car out of the garage and I went to see my old lady, who lives alone in a little house at the other end of town. Twice, I made a point of passing in front of the Hotel de l'Europe to look up at the windows. Angèle had said she was giving Martine number 78. I had no idea where the room was, but there was one corner room on the second floor where the curtains were drawn and I gazed up at it with emotion.

I went into the Poker-Bar, your Honour, the place I told you about, where I almost never set foot; and that morning I drank a glass of white wine, which – I had had nothing to eat – seemed to burn a hole in my stomach.

'Boquet hasn't been in yet?'

'After the night they spent, he and his gang, there's not a chance of his appearing before five or six o'clock this evening. They were still here when the first Paris train left . . .'

When I got home, Armande was telephoning the dressmaker to announce that she had the buttons and to make an appointment. I didn't see my mother. I was able to reach my office and sluice out my patients one after the other.

More and more, as the time passed, I had the impression that I was wasting my life. The day was grey, joyless. The window of the little office in which I write out prescriptions overlooks the garden, where the dark shrubs were quietly dripping. As for the window in my consulting room it was of ground glass and the electric light had to be kept on all day.

Little by little an idea was taking root in my mind which at first had seemed to me absurd, but which became less so as time passed, as patient succeeded patient. Didn't I have two colleagues right here in La Roche-sur-Yon, with no larger clientele than mine, who had a nurse to assist them? Without counting the specialists, like my friend Dambois, all of whom had nurses.

I had begun to detest Raoul Boquet and yet, your Honour, I can truly say – for a doctor is in a position to know such things – that as a man I had no cause to envy him. Quite the contrary! And just because he is rotten with physical taints, I got all the more furious at the thought of any kind of intimacy between him and Martine.

Eleven o'clock, you understand? Eleven thirty. A poor kid – I can still see him – with mumps and an enormous bandage around his head. Then a whitlow to be lanced. Others. There were always others who took the place of the preceding ones on the benches.

She would not come. It was impossible to believe that she would come. And why, will you tell me, should she come?

A work casualty was brought to me in a small truck because I am doctor for the insurance company. With a swagger, the man pointed to his crushed thumb, saying:

'Chop it off, for Christ's sake! Go ahead, chop it off! I bet you haven't the guts to chop it off. Am I going to have to do it myself?'

When I saw him out, sweat was pouring over my eyes

so that I could hardly see and I almost called the next patient before I noticed her, dressed in the same dark tailored suit she had worn the day before, with the same hat, sitting at the very end of the benches.

God, how stupid to have to use the same words which have served so long to express banalities! My throat contracted. As tight as an artery tied with catgut. What else can I say, how else describe it?

My throat in a knot, I crossed the room instead of standing as I always did with one hand holding the door open.

She told me later that I was terrifying. It is possible. I had been so afraid. And, I promise you, I didn't worry at that moment about what the five or six patients who were waiting their turn, perhaps for hours, would think.

I planted myself in front of her. This also I learned from her. I no longer tried to control myself, I said, my teeth clenched, almost menacingly:

'Come in . . .'

Could I really have looked so terrifying? I was too frightened for that. I had been too frightened. I did not yet feel reassured. I had to wait for her to go through the door, and to close it.

Then, it seems, I heaved a sigh as hoarse as a groan and letting my arms, grown lifeless, fall to my sides, I articulated:

'You came . . .'

At the trial, what I was most severely blamed for was having brought a woman, having brought my mistress into our home. I think in their eyes that was my greatest crime and that they would even, at a pinch, have forgiven my having committed murder. But bringing

Martine face to face with Armande, that made them so indignant that they were at a loss to qualify my conduct.

What would you have done, your Honour? Could I have gone away then and there? Would that have seemed more normal? Just like that, the very first day, without giving it a thought?

Did I even know where we were headed? There was only one thing I knew, just one, and that was that I could not live without her and that I felt a physical pain, as violent as that of my most afflicted patients, the moment she was not near me, the moment I no longer saw her, no longer heard her.

It was suddenly a total vacuum.

Is this so very extraordinary? Am I the only man to have been caught in this vortex?

Am I the first man to have hated as I hated anyone who might approach her in my absence?

One might have thought so to hear those gentlemen of the law, who sometimes looked at me with indignation, sometimes with pity. More often with indignation.

Note that when I saw her in the light of my office, I was almost disillusioned. She had again the brittle look of the girl of the previous day, the look she had had *before*. Perhaps because she was nervous, ill at ease, she affected her old assurance of a habitué of smart bars.

I sought some trace of what had happened to us and found none.

No matter. Even that way, I was not going to let her go. I would not be free for another hour at least. I could have asked her to come back later. But I didn't want her to go away from the house. I didn't even want to leave her alone in my house. Someone must guard her.

'Listen ... you are going to lunch here at the house

... Yes, you are ... No need to mention that we met yesterday, for Armande is naturally suspicious and my mother even more so ... For both of them, you came to me this morning with a letter of introduction from Dr Artari of Paris, whom I know slightly and whom my wife does not know ...'

She was not convinced, but she felt that it was not the moment to cross me.

'You can talk about Boquet ... that would even be wiser ... But you should imply that you have been working for a doctor – Dr Artari, for instance ...'

I was in such a hurry to arrange all this that my hand was already on the knob of the door leading to the house.

'My name is Englebert,' she said, 'Martine Englebert ... I am Belgian – from Liège ...'

She smiled. It was true, I did not know her family name and that would have been embarrassing when I introduced her.

'You'll see ... Leave everything to me ...'

I was wild. I'm sorry if you find it ridiculous, your Honour. I had brought her to my home. It was almost a trap. I felt a little as if I were appropriating her and it wouldn't have taken much for the idea of locking her up to have occurred to me. I could hear one of my patients coughing in the waiting-room.

'Come ...'

Lightly, I touched my lips to her lips. I went ahead. We were in my front hall, the drawing-room on the left; the smell that floated in the air was the smell of my house and she was in my house.

I caught sight of Mama in the drawing-room and I rushed over to her.

'Listen, Mama ... I want to introduce a young girl who was sent to me by Dr Artari, a physician I know in Paris ... She has come to work in La Roche where she doesn't know a soul ... I have invited her to have lunch with us ...'

Mama, as she rose, dropped her ball of wool.

'I entrust her to your care. I must return to my patients ... Tell Babette to be sure to give us a good luncheon ...'

Was I on the point of singing when I left? I wonder if I wasn't actually humming when I closed the door of my office. I had the impression of having won such a victory, and, to tell the truth, I was proud of my cunning! Think of it, she was under Mama's protection. No man could talk to her while they were together. And Martine, whether she wanted to or not, would continue to live in my atmosphere.

Even if Armande came downstairs. I didn't know whether she had gone out or not, but it would not be long before they found themselves face to face.

All right! Armande would guard her for me too. In high spirits, with a feeling of relief I had never known before, I opened the door into the waiting-room.

Next! And, once more, next! Open your mouth. Cough. Breathe. Don't breathe.

She was there, not ten yards away from me. When I went near the little door at the back I could hear the murmur of voices. It was too confused for me to recognize her voice, but she was nevertheless there.

I think you were in court when the prosecutor, raising his arms to heaven, addressed, not me, but some mysterious power:

'What could this man have hoped for?'

I smiled. My hideous smile, you know! I smiled and I said very low, but distinctly enough so that one of my two guards heard me:

'To be happy . . .'

In reality, I never asked myself the question. I was lucid enough, in spite of everything, to foresee all the complications, the endless difficulties.

Don't talk to me of the primrose path of vice, as some imbecile did at my trial. There was no primrose path. There was no vice.

There was a man who did what he did because he could not do otherwise and that's that. He did it because what was suddenly at stake, after forty years, was his own happiness, which nobody had ever bothered about before, not even himself – a happiness he had not sought, which had been given him gratuitously and which he had not the right to throw away.

Forgive me, your Honour, if I shock you. But, after all, I too have the right to talk. And I have this advantage over the others, that I know what I'm talking about. I have paid the price. They have never paid anything, and therefore I do not admit their right to meddle in what they know nothing about.

It can't be helped if you, like the others, pronounce the word cynicism. At the point I've reached it is of no importance. Cynicism, so be it, if you like. Since that morning, in fact, perhaps since some moment, I don't know just when, of that night, I accepted in advance everything that might happen.

Everything, your Honour. Do you hear?

Everything except losing her. Everything, except to have her go away, to live without her, to feel again that appalling pain in my chest.

I had no preconceived plan. It is false to say that that morning when I introduced her to my mother I was bringing my concubine – God, how certain words give away the people who use them – under the conjugal roof.

I had to find a shelter for her at once. For the rest, it could be decided later. The important thing was to keep her from having any contact with Boquet, or with any other man.

I continued seeing patients, my soul at peace. When I entered the drawing-room, the three women were sitting there like ladies paying calls, and Martine was holding my youngest daughter on her lap.

'I have had the pleasure of meeting your wife,' she said without the least irony, without any kind of intention, simply because she had to say something.

There were three little glasses of port on the table and, in the centre, our beautiful cut-glass carafe. The drawing-room was really pretty that morning with the tulle curtains hiding the dreary greyness that enveloped the city.

'Mlle Englebert has been telling us all about her family ...'

Armande gave me a little sign I knew very well, which meant that she wanted to speak to me privately.

'I must go down to the cellar and pick out a special bottle of wine,' I said.

And then, without the least hypocrisy I assure you, gaily, because suddenly I felt gay:

'Tell me, Mademoiselle, what wines do you prefer, white or red, dry or sweet?'

'Dry, that is if Mme Alavoine ...'

I left the room. Armande followed me.

'Do you think we can leave her at the hotel until she finds an apartment? She went to the Europe this morning. If Artari recommended her to you . . . What does he say in his letter?'

I hadn't thought of that. I should have a letter.

'He asks me to have an eye on her for a while . . . He doesn't like the position offered her at Boquet's, but we can look into that later . . .'

'If I knew that it would only be for a few days, I would ask her to stay . . . She could have the green room . . .'

There you are, your Honour! The green room! Next to Mama's, separated from mine by my daughters'.

'Do as you think best.'

Poor Martine, who must have heard us whispering in the hall, not knowing, never dreaming of the turn things were taking. Mama was talking and she pretended to be listening while straining her ears to hear what we were saying, more dead than alive.

She would not see Boquet, she would not work for him, that was decided. I didn't lose any time, you see. It was destiny, your Honour, it was a force that was beyond us.

I was so grateful to Armande that I looked at her during luncheon as I had probably never looked at her before, with real affection. A perfect luncheon which Mama had been allowed to superintend. We weren't hungry, Martine and I, and ate without paying much attention. Our eyes laughed. We were gay. Everybody was gay, your Honour, as by a miracle.

'Presently, my husband will go to the hotel to pick up your baggage. But I insist . . . I don't think it will be difficult to find a furnished apartment. After lunch I'll do a little telephoning . . .'

We wanted to go to the hotel together. We already felt the need of being alone. We dared not go about it too precipitately. The suggestion could not come from me.

It was then I saw how artful Martine was – I almost said, what a hussy she was. The ladies were finishing their coffee. I was about to leave.

'Would you mind, Mme Alavoine, if I went to the hotel too?'

Then lowering her voice, as though in confidence:

'There are a few little things lying round the room and . . .'

Armande had understood. Little feminine secrets, by Jove! Little modesties! It wasn't for a great brute like me to be going into a young girl's room, handling her lingerie, her personal possessions.

I can still hear Armande, lowering her voice to advise me, while Martine was putting on her funny little hat in front of the mirror in the hall:

'Let her go up alone . . . It's more tactful . . . You would embarrass her . . .'

The car, my car. The two of us inside, I at the wheel, Martine beside me, and my city, the streets I walked along every day.

'It's marvellous . . .' I said.

'Doesn't it frighten you a little bit? . . . Do you think we should accept?'

She did not make fun of Armande now. She felt ashamed in front of her.

But no one in the world could have stopped me now. I went up with her. Even before closing the door I took her in my arms, almost smothering her in my embrace and I literally devoured her mouth. The bed had not been made. But the idea of possessing her at that moment never occurred to me. Granted, it was important. It was while I was hugging her like an animal that I understood. But this was not the moment.

There were other things to accomplish immediately.

I had to take her home again, your Honour, and never more triumphantly has bridegroom taken home his bride.

I had to moderate the light in my eyes, the radiance of my whole being.

'I have telephoned already,' Armande announced, 'and I have an address.'

Then, taking me aside:

'It would be better if I went with her . . .'

How I agreed with her! Just so there was someone to guard her! And it seemed perfectly natural to me that it should be either my mother or Armande.

Duplicity, hypocrisy?

No, your Honour, no, no, no! You can let those who do not know say that, you who may soon know, you who, unless I am very much mistaken, will know one day.

The irresistible force of life, that's all of life which had been given to me at last, given to me who, for so long, had been only a man without a shadow.

Chapter Seven

There isn't an incident, a word, a gesture of those days that I have forgotten and yet it would be impossible for me to reconstruct the events in their chronological order. It's more of a tangle of memories, each with its own life, each forming a whole, and it is often the more meaningless ones that stand out in the sharpest outlines.

For instance, I see myself that afternoon, about six o'clock, opening the door into the Poker-Bar. In the morning I still had a ghost of a reason for going there. But now that I had decided that Martine, no matter what happened, should not become Raoul Boquet's secretary ...

And, you see, I may even be mistaken: all at once, I wonder if it wasn't the following day. I can still feel the icy wind rushing up under my overcoat when I got out of the car, and see, in a row and slanting gently down-hill, the few lights along the street, shop lights power-less to snare a single customer in such a squall.

Right beside me, the creamy and slightly rosy light of the bar and, as soon as I opened the door, an atmosphere of pleasant warmth and cordiality. There were so many people in the smoke of the pipes and cigarettes that the newcomer had the impression of being snubbed, of not having been taken into the secret. If the streets were deserted, if only a few wretches roamed them aimlessly, it was because everybody had met everybody else at the Poker-Bar and at other places of the sort, behind closed doors where they couldn't be seen.

What had I come for? Nothing. I was there simply to look at Boquet. Not even to defy him, for what had I to say to him? Just to look at a man who, one night, when he was drunk, had met Martine, had spoken to her – before me – bought her a drink and had almost become her boss. Would he have become her lover into the bargain?

I didn't speak to him. He was too drunk for that and he didn't even notice I was there.

It is here in prison, a perfect place for thinking, that this fact has struck me: almost all my memories of the holiday season in the Vendée, as far back as I can remember, are memories of clear weather, a somewhat greenish-yellow light, glossy, like certain coloured postcards, rarely with snow, almost always a dry cold. But that year – last year, your Honour – I see only dark days where, in most offices, the lights were turned on, the pavements black under the rain, black windy nights that began too early, and those scattered lights in the city which give to the provinces a character at once so intimate and so sad.

That is what reminded me of Caen. But I had no time to dwell on the past. I lived in such a continual tension that I wonder how, if only physically, I was able to stand it. Above all, I wonder how those who saw me failed to understand what was happening to me.

How could certain persons have seen me coming and going without suspecting that I was living through an extraordinary moment? Was I really the only one to be conscious of it? Several times Armande looked at me with anxious curiosity. Not anxious for me. Anxious because she could not bear not to understand, because instinctively she resisted anything that threatened the order she herself had established around her.

Luck was with me. At that time we were having, almost simultaneously, an epidemic of grippe and of scarlatina, which kept me breathless from morning to night and sometimes from night to morning. The waiting-room was never empty. Under the glass porch there were always a dozen or more open umbrellas dripping along the wall, and the floors were constantly streaked with water and mud from all the wet feet. The telephone never stopped ringing. My more astute patients and my friends would come to the front door and would be circumspectly shown into my office between two ordinary patients. I joyously welcomed all this work, I needed this feverish activity to excuse my own feverish excitement.

It was almost impossible for Martine and me to see each other alone. But she was in my house and that was enough for me. I would often make noises just so that she would hear me, so that she would never cease to be conscious of my presence. In the morning, I adopted the habit of humming while I shaved and she understood so well that a few moments later I would hear her singing in her room.

Mama, I'd be willing to swear, understood this too. She said nothing. She let nothing appear. It is true that she had no reason to love Armande. Quite the contrary. Is it indecent of me to speculate still further and to imagine a certain inner jubilation in my mother as, little by little, she made these discoveries which she kept strictly to herself?

At all events, as I learned later, in fact she herself has admitted it, she had guessed everything after the second or third day, and it disturbs me a little now to think that things which I thought so secret, which love alone rendered acceptable, have had a lucid and silent witness.

It was in the morning of the third day, during my office hours, that Armande, ordering a taxi so as not to bother me, took Martine to Mme Debeurre's, where she had found a room with a kitchen. The second, the third day – it all seemed so long to me then. And although it hasn't been even a year yet, how long ago it seems! So much longer, for instance, than my daughter's diphtheria or my marriage to Armande ten years ago, because during those ten years nothing vital happened.

For Martine and me, on the contrary, the world was changing from hour to hour, things were happening so rapidly that we did not always have time to keep each other informed of events or of our own evolution.

I had said to her hurriedly in passing:

'You're not going to Boquet's. I've found something else. Just leave it to me . . .'

In spite of my assurance, I did not really feel certain, and, in any case, I thought it would take weeks if not months. I was certain of it without being certain, I wanted it without knowing how I should go about it, there were so many obstacles in the way of such a project.

What could be done in the meantime? I couldn't even keep Martine, who was down to her last franc, and would not have let me anyway.

Forty, fifty patients a day, your Honour, and not only in my office but in town, in the suburbs, some in the country, so that because of our bad roads in the Vendée I practically lived in riding breeches and boots.

Add to all this, preparations for Christmas, presents for the children and for the grown-ups, the Christmas tree and ornaments to be bought, and the crèche, used in former years, which I had not yet had time to have repaired.

Is it any wonder that I am confused about the exact order of events? But I remember clearly that it was ten o'clock in the morning and that I had a patient in my office wearing a black shawl, when I gave myself a deadline of a few weeks – three weeks, I think – to bring Armande around to my way of thinking.

But that very day at noon Babette knocked on the door of my office, which meant that my bouillon was waiting for me. For in times of unusual stress I was in the habit of interrupting my consultations for a few moments to drink a bowl of hot bouillon in the kitchen. Armande's idea, as a matter of fact. When I think back, I perceive that everything I did was regulated by Armande, and so naturally that I did not even realize it.

I was really exhausted. My hand shook a little from nervousness as I picked up the bowl. My wife happened to be in the kitchen making a cake at the time.

'Things can't go on like this,' I said, taking advantage of the fact that it would be impossible to engage in a long discussion and that she would hardly have time to reply. 'If I were sure that young girl was dependable, I think I'd engage her as an assistant . . .'

But all this, all these preoccupations I have just told you about, were, your Honour, what counted the least. The real cause of my feverish state lay elsewhere.

You see I was at the painful, the important stage of the discovery.

I did not know Martine. I was hungry to know her. It was not curiosity, but an almost physical need. And every hour lost was painful, physically painful too. So many things can happen in an hour! In spite of my dearth of imagination I thought of all the possible catastrophes.

And the worst one of all was that from one moment to the next she would not be the same.

I was conscious of the miracle that had occurred, and there was no reason for the miracle to continue.

We simply had to learn to know one another at once,

no matter what the cost, to complete our total knowledge, go to the end of what, without wanting to, we had started at Nantes.

Only then, I said to myself, would I be happy. Only then would I be able to look at her with calm and confident eyes. Would I then, perhaps, be able to leave her for a few hours without trembling with suspense?

I had a thousand questions to ask her, a thousand things to tell her. I could only talk to her on rare occasions during the day and always in the presence of my mother or Armande.

We had begun at the end. It was urgent, it was indispensable to fill the voids which gave me a sort of vertigo.

For example, just to hold her hand without saying a word ...

If I slept at all during this period I have no recollection of it, and I am sure it must have been very little. I lived like a sleep-walker. My eyes were glassy, my eyelids tingled, my skin was too tender – the signs that one has reached the end of one's endurance. I can see myself in the middle of the night, biting my pillow in a rage, thinking of her sleeping only a few feet away from me.

At night she would cough a few times before going to sleep, which was her way of sending me a final message. I would cough in answer, and I'd be willing to swear that my mother understood this coughing language too.

I don't know what would have happened if things had dragged on much longer, if they had taken place as I had envisaged. One is apt to imagine that nerves can snag like violin strings which are too tightly stretched.

This is absurd, of course. But I think one fine day I would have been capable, at table or in the drawing-room, in the street or no matter where, of suddenly starting to yell for no apparent reason.

Armande said, without making any of the objections I had expected:

'Wait at least until after Christmas before speaking to her. We'll have to discuss it first, you and I . . .'

I am obliged to give you a few more professional details. You know that in the provinces we doctors are still in the habit, for our most important patients, of waiting until the end of the year before sending our bill. It is a doctor's nightmare. It was mine. Naturally we do not always keep an exact account of our visits. It is necessary to go over our appointment book, page by page, make an approximate estimate that won't startle our patient too much.

Up to that time Armande had always undertaken this task. I had never had to ask her, for she liked such minute and orderly exercises and, moreover, ever since our marriage she had quite naturally taken charge of my financial affairs, to such an extent that I was reduced to asking her for money when I wanted to buy anything.

At night, as I was undressing, she would collect the money I took out of my pockets, the amount I had received in cash for my visits during the day, and would even frown sometimes and ask for an explanation. I would have to go over again my round of visits, remember all the patients I had seen, those who had paid and those who had not paid.

This year, nevertheless, Armande complained of being overwhelmed with work, and I took advantage of a moment when I saw her plunged in her accounts to say:

'She could also help you – little by little, getting the hang of it . . .'

Who knows if it wasn't a trait of Armande's character which so hastened matters that I was the first to be surprised? She has always liked to manage things, whether the house or anything else. If she really loved her first husband, if, as I was always being told, she was wonderful to him, wasn't it because he was ill, because he was at her mercy, could count on nobody but her, and because she could treat him like a child?

To dominate was a need of her nature, and I don't believe it was through petty vanity or even pride. It was, I think, rather to preserve and increase the feeling that she had about herself and that she needed to keep her equilibrium.

She had not been able to live with her father, for the very reason that her father was not impressed by her and continued to treat her as a little girl, to live his own life just as though she were not in the same house. As time went on, I wonder if she would not have fallen ill or become neurasthenic.

For ten years she had under her thumb, first of all, me, who had not tried to resist and who always yielded for the sake of peace, to the point of asking her opinion even about buying a necktie or the smallest instrument of my profession – to the point of accounting to her for all my movements. There was also my mother who had yielded in her own way, who had retired to the place assigned her by Armande while still safeguarding her personality, who, it is true, obeyed because she felt that she was not at home, but remained impermeable to her daughter-in-law's influence.

Then there were my daughters, naturally more pliable. The maid. A servant who had a 'character of her own' did not last long in our house, no more than one who did not admire my wife. Finally there were all our friends, or practically all of them, all the young women of our circle who came to ask her advice. This had happened so often that Armande no longer waited to be asked, but offered her advice of her own accord on every occasion; and people had told her so often that she was never wrong, and it had become accepted as such a foregone conclusion in certain milieus of La Roche, that she could no longer conceive of a contradiction being possible.

You see why it was a stroke of genius, mentioning those end-of-the-year bills. It was putting Martine under her thumb, it was one more human being coming under her domination.

'The girl seems quite intelligent,' she murmured, 'but I wonder if she is methodical enough? . . .'

Because of this, your Honour, the evening I went to see Martine for the first time in her new apartment at Mme Debeurre's, I had two pieces of good news to announce. First that my wife invited her to spend Christmas Eve with us, something I should never have dared hope. And second, that before the end of the year, in less than ten days, she would, in all likelihood, be my assistant.

In spite of this, all afternoon I had the sensation of being at a loose end. Martine was no longer in the house. At luncheon she was not at the table, and I almost began to doubt my memories, to ask myself if the day before she had really been seated there opposite me, between Armande and my mother.

She was alone in a house which I didn't know, except from the outside. She was beyond my control. She was seeing other people. She spoke to them no doubt, smiled at them.

And I couldn't rush right over to her. I had to make my round of visits, come back to my office twice for urgent cases.

One more professional detail, your Honour. Forgive me, but it is necessary. When I had to go to see patients in town, I was supposed, before leaving, like most doctors, to list the names of the patients I was about to visit, so that in case of an emergency I could be reached by telephone at one house or another. In this way every moment of my time could be checked. This was one of the established rules Armande insisted upon above all others. If, as I was leaving, I forgot to write down all the addresses in the notebook, kept in the hall for the purpose, she was quick to notice it and I would not have started my car before she was knocking on the window to call me back.

How many times in my life have I been called back like that! I couldn't say anything. She was right.

I am still not sure today if it was through jealousy she acted in this way, and I believe, without believing, that it was. Do you want me to explain what I think, once for all?

There was never any question of love between us. You know what happened before our marriage. Love for her, if love there was, and I am willing to accord her that, was in the past; it was for her first husband who had died.

Our marriage was a marriage of reason. She liked my house. She liked a certain kind of life I could give her.

As for me, I had my two daughters and no one but my old Mama to look after them, which did not seem to me desirable.

Did she come to love me later on? This question has bothered me in the last few months and especially lately. Formerly I should have replied no, without hesitation. I was convinced that she loved no one but herself, that she had never loved anyone but herself.

If she was jealous, it was of her influence over me, you understand. She was afraid of seeing me break the leash she held in her hands.

I used to think all this and many other things, for, even before Martine, I had my hours of revolt.

Now that I am on the other side and that I feel so detached from everything, I am much more indulgent, or understanding.

Take, for example, when she was on the witness-stand: she might very well have made me bristle by her attitude, by her calm, by her self-assurance. You felt – and she wanted you to feel – that she harboured no resentment towards me, that she was ready, if I should be acquitted, to take me back and to nurse me as a sick man.

That too can be explained by her need of dominating, her need of having a more and more exalted idea of herself, of her character.

Well, I no longer think so. Without speaking of love, for now I know what the word means, I am convinced that, in a sense, she really loved me a little, the way she loves my daughters.

And she has always been perfect towards my daughters. Everybody at La Roche will tell you that she has acted, and still does act, just like their own mother. She has adopted them to such an extent that I have gradually and unconsciously lost interest in them.

I ask their pardon. I am their father. How can I explain to them that it is just because, as a father, I was left too little place?

Armande has loved me as she loved them, calmly and with an indulgent severity. I have never been her husband, much less her lover. I was someone she had taken under her charge, for whom she had assumed the responsibility, in whom, consequently, she felt she had proprietary rights.

Including that of regulating all my comings and goings. That I believe is the secret of her jealousy.

Mine, damn it all, when I knew Martine, was of a different sort, and I wouldn't want anyone to know jealousy like that. I don't know why that day, more than any other, remains in my mind as a day of lights and darkness. I had the impression of spending my time going from the cold obscurity of the street into the warm luminosity of interiors. From outside I saw soft lighted windows, golden shades. I covered a few yards of darkness, I removed my wet coat, and for a moment I participated in the life of a strange fireside, conscious all the time of the darkness on the other side of the window panes . . .

God, what a state I was in!

'She is alone in her apartment. Fat Mme Debeurre will surely go up to see her . . .'

I clung to this reassuring thought. Mme Debeurre is a woman of uncertain age who has had misfortunes. Her husband was a tax collector. She lived not far from the station in a rather pretty red brick house of two stories, with three steps leading up to a front door of polished oak overloaded with brasses. During her whole married life she wanted to have children, and had consulted me on the subject; she had seen all my colleagues, she had gone to Nantes, even to Paris, receiving always the same reply.

Her husband had got himself killed by a train in the station of La Roche not two hundred yards from their house, and since then, dreading the loneliness, she had rented her second-floor apartment furnished.

To think of my being content at the thought that a Mme Debeurre, after my mother and Armande, was with Martine!

A dozen times I was on the point of going to see her between two calls. I also passed in front of the Poker-Bar. I had even less reason for going in now, and yet I almost did.

We dined to the accompaniment of forks and plates. I still had a few calls to make in town.

'Perhaps I'll drop in to see if that young girl has everything she needs. I have to write to Artari tomorrow and tell him how she's getting on.'

I feared some opposition, some objection. Armande, although she must have heard, said nothing, and my mother alone gave a rather too insistent look.

It is a wide avenue. It runs along the old ramparts. A neighbourhood of barracks. There aren't more than two or three shops to throw a rectangle of light on the sidewalk.

I was feverish, my heart pounded. I saw the house with a light on the ground floor and another light upstairs. I rang the bell. I heard Mme Debeurre's slippers flip-flapping down the hall.

'Oh, it's you, Doctor ... The young lady has just come in ...'

I went upstairs four steps at a time. I knocked. While I stared at the line of light under the door, a placid voice bade me come in.

There was a blue silk shade over the lamp, and under the shade smoke was curling.

Why did I scowl? Why did I have that empty feeling? No doubt I was expecting immediately to have Martine standing there, her body pressed against mine. I had to look all around the room before I saw her lying on the bed in her clothes, smiling, a cigarette in her mouth.

Then, instead of rushing over to embrace her, instead of announcing my two pieces of good news, which I had kept repeating to myself all the way, brutally I asked:

'What are you doing there?'

Never in my life had I spoken like that. I have never been domineering. I have always been afraid of shocking, of wounding. My voice surprised me.

Smiling, she replied, but perhaps already with a shade of anxiety in her eyes:

'I was taking a rest while waiting for you to come ...'

'You didn't know that I was coming ...'

'But I did ...'

What irritated me, I think, was to find her looking exactly as I had seen her at the American bar in Nantes, with her cover-girl smile, which I was beginning to hate.

'You went out?'

'I had to eat. Here, there was nothing ready ...'

I felt like being cruel to her, I, who had been so patient with Armande, whom I did not love.

It was so simple to go over to her, to kiss her, to fold

her in my arms. I had been thinking about it all day. I had lived that moment a hundred times in advance and everything was happening differently. I remained standing, without even taking off my overcoat, with my boots dripping on the carpet.

'Where did you have dinner?'

'In a little restaurant, called the Green Oak, somebody told me about . . .'

'Not Mme Debeurre at any rate . . .'

I knew the Green Oak. It is not a restaurant for strangers, who would have difficulty finding it, tucked away at the back of a courtyard which looks like the courtyard of a farm. It is practically a pension, frequented by bachelor functionaries of the city, habitués, and a few travelling salesmen who pass through La Roche periodically.

'You had a cocktail, I'll bet . . .'

She was no longer smiling. She was sitting on the edge of the bed and was looking at me with an anxious hurt expression, like a little girl who wonders why she is being scolded.

After all, she didn't know me yet. She had no idea what my true character was, what our love would be.

And yet, your Honour, that love, whatever it would be, she accepted. Do you understand what that means? I myself understood it only much later.

I was tense, and haunted by a fixed idea, like a man who has drunk too much.

'You went to the Poker-Bar . . .'

I had no idea she had. But I had been so afraid of it that I made the statement feeling almost certain that I was not wrong.

'I think that is what it's called . . . I couldn't stay shut up all day ... I had to have some air ... I took a little walk ...'

'And you wanted a drink ...'

Damn it all! Wasn't everything I knew about her mixed up with bars?

'You couldn't wait, could you, to wallow in your filthy atmosphere again?'

Because, suddenly, that atmosphere was what I hated most in the whole world. Those high stools where she perched with her legs crossed so naturally! And the cigarette-case she took out of her bag, the cigarette – the cigarette stained with lipstick which she couldn't do without any more than she could do without cocktails which she would watch being mixed ... and after that letting her eyes wander from one man to another, seeking attention – hungry for attention ...

I seized her wrists, not even knowing what I was doing. I jerked her to her feet.

'Admit that you were missing it already ... Admit that you wanted to see Bouquet ... Go on, admit it ...'

I was gripping her wrists hard enough to hurt her. I no longer knew if I loved her or if I hated her.

'Admit it! ... I'm so sure I'm right ... You just had to go and start something with him ...'

She could have denied it. That is what I expected. I think I should have been satisfied. She hung her head. She stammered:

'I wonder ... Perhaps ...'

'You wanted to play around with him, didn't you?'

I gave her wrists several hard jerks and I saw that I was hurting her, that she was frightened, that automatically her eyes sought the door.

I think from that day, from that moment, I was ready to strike her. And yet I was moved. I was filled with pity for her, she was so pale, her face drawn with anguish and fatigue. Her cigarette had fallen on the carpet and she was trying to put it out with her foot, for fear of fire. I noticed her movement and it increased my rage to think that she could, at a moment like this, bother about such a trifle.

'You had to have a man, didn't you?'

She shook her head.

'Admit it . . .'

'No . . .'

'You had to have a drink . . .'

'Perhaps . . .'

'You had to have attention . . . You have to have men paying attention to you all the time and you are capable of stopping a policeman on the street with any old excuse, just so he'll make love to you.'

'You're hurting me . . .'

'You're nothing but a whore . . .'

As I uttered the word, I jerked her wrists even harder than before and sent her rolling on the floor. She did not make a sound. She remained there with one arm crooked in front of her face in fear of the blows she was expecting.

'Get up . . .'

She obeyed me slowly, staring at me as though terror-stricken, but there was no trace of hate or resentment in her eyes.

Littly by little I realized all this and I was stupefied. I had just behaved like a beast and she accepted it. I had just insulted her and she did not resent it.

She stammered something like:

'Don't hurt me . . .'

At that I stood motionless, I said in a voice which must have sounded much the same as before:

'Come here . . .'

She hesitated an instant. Finally she came towards me, still protecting her face with her arm. She was sure that I was going to strike her. But she came, your Honour. That is the point, she came!

And we had met each other for the first time three days before.

I had no idea of beating her. I wanted her to come of her own accord. When she was close to me, I opened my arms and I pressed her to my breast so hard she could scarcely breathe, while tears filled my eyes.

I stammered in her ear, all warm against my cheek:

'Forgive me . . .'

We were standing in a close embrace a few steps from the bed.

'Did you see him?'

'Who?'

All this was no more than a whisper.

'You know perfectly well . . .'

'No . . . he wasn't there . . .'

'And if he had been there?'

'I would have told him that I was not going to be his secretary . . .'

'But you would have had a drink with him . . .'

'Perhaps . . .'

She was speaking low as at confession. I could not see her eyes, which must have been looking over my shoulder.

'Who was it you talked to?'

'No one . . .'

'You're lying . . . Someone must have told you about the Green Oak . . .'

'That's so. But I don't know his name . . .'

'He asked you to have a drink, didn't he?'

'I think so . . . Yes . . .'

Suddenly I was sad, your Honour. A tender sadness. I had the impression that I was holding a sick child in my arms. She was a liar. She was depraved.

But just the same, she had come to me when she thought I was going to hurt her. She in turn stammered:

'Forgive me . . .'

Then these words, which I shall never forget, these words which more than anything else came like an echo from her childhood:

'I won't do it again . . .'

She too wanted to cry, but she did not cry. She kept very still for fear of unleashing my demons again, and then I drew her gently towards the bed which still held the imprint of her body.

Again she stammered, perhaps with a certain astonishment:

'You want to?'

I wanted to, yes. But not as at Nantes. I wanted to feel that she was mine. I wanted her flesh to mingle intimately with mine, and it was slowly, with full consciousness, my throat tight with emotion, that I took possession of her.

I understood right away what was worrying her, the reason for that look of anxiety in her eyes. She was afraid of offending me. She was baffled by the calmness of my caress which seemed free from voluptuous pleasure.

After a long moment I heard a whisper:

'Should I? . . .'

I said no. It wasn't her panting body striving for a deliverance she could not find, it wasn't her haggard eyes, her mouth open as though to utter a cry of despair that I desired today. All that, in fact, I had decided never to desire again. That was what the others had had. That was the old Martine, the Martine of cocktails, cigarettes and bars.

That evening I never considered her pleasure. Nor my own. It was not pleasure I was looking for.

What I wanted was, deliberately and with, I repeat, full consciousness of my act, to impregnate her with my substance, and my emotion was that of a man living through the most solemn hour of his life.

Once and for all I accepted my responsibilities. Not only mine but hers. I was taking her life in charge, both her present and her past, and that is why, your Honour, I held her almost sadly in my arms.

She remained calm and serious. As soon as she felt me melting into her, she turned her head slightly on the pillow, probably to hide her tears. Her hand sought mine, pressed my fingers with the same deliberateness and tenderness as mine when I possessed her.

We lay there for a long time like that in silence, and now we heard Mme Debeurre moving about downstairs, intentionally making a lot of noise, annoyed, probably, by our long tête-à-tête.

These perfectly transparent wiles of hers ended by amusing us, for the good woman, every now and then, would come to the foot of the stairs and stand there listening, as though worried not to hear our voices. Was it because she had heard Martine's fall?

Quietly I disengaged myself.

'I almost forgot to tell you ... You are invited to spend Christmas Eve at the house ...'

And I had imagined myself shouting the words in an outburst of joy! But here I was speaking of it in the simplest way in the world, as though of some fortuitous event.

'Another thing. After the holidays, probably the day after New Year's, you will work with me as my assistant.'

We had already gone beyond that.

'I have to go ...'

She rose. She smoothed her hair a little before coming up to me, putting her two arms on my shoulders and, in an artless gesture, holding up her lips to mine.

'Good night, Charles ...'

'Good night, Martine ...'

The throatiness of her voice that evening moved me to the depth of my being. To hear it once more, I repeated:

'Good night, Martine ...'

'Good night, Charles ...'

I took another look around the room and moved away. I stammered:

'Tomorrow ...'

She did not ask me what time, and that meant she would be waiting for me all day, because in the future she would always be waiting for me.

I had to leave quickly, for my emotion was too much for me and I did not want to give in to it again. I needed to be alone, to be once more in the cool darkness of the street, the solitude of the deserted avenues.

She opened the door for me. I don't know how we managed to break away from one another. I had already gone down a few steps when she repeated, in exactly the same tone of voice as before, like an incantation – and indeed, from that evening on, it became a kind of incantation:

'Good night, Charles . . .'

Little did we care for Mme Debeurre spying on us behind her half-open door.

'Good night, Martine . . .'

'I won't go there any more, you know . . .'

I rushed out. I had just time to reach my car and to slip in behind the wheel before bursting into tears, and as I drove along, the street-lamps and the headlights of the few cars I passed were so blurred that I had to draw up to the kerb and stop for some time.

A policeman came up, looked in, recognized me.

'Your car break down, Doctor?'

I didn't want him to see my face. I took my appointment book out of my pocket. I pretended to be consulting it.

'No . . . just looking up an address . . .'

Chapter Eight

We spent a quiet Christmas among ourselves – Armande, my mother, my daughters, Martine, my friend Frachon and I. Frachon is a bald-headed bachelor who has no family at La Roche – one of those bachelors, in fact, who takes his meals at the Green Oak – and whom for years we always invited for Christmas Eve. Armande received a piece of jewellery, a platinum clip which she had wanted for some time. She seldom wears jewellery but she likes to own it, and I think the first time I ever saw her lose her composure, even to the point of actually weeping, was the day that, wanting to offer her a little present of no importance, I had bought her some imitation pearls. I don't say that she is avaricious. Even if she were, I should not think myself justified in resenting it or blaming her, for everyone has his own vice. She likes to possess beautiful things, valuable things, even if she never takes them out of her drawer.

I had bought nothing of value for Martine for fear of attracting attention. I even pushed caution so far as to ask my wife to buy two or three pairs of silk stockings to give her.

This very peaceful Christmas was invoked in court. I don't know if you were present. The prosecutor stigmatized my *cynicism*, accusing me of having, by *ignoble and hypocritical means, insinuated my concubine into the family circle.*

I did not protest. I never once protested, and yet many times I had the distinct sensation that these men – including my own lawyers, who for me were birds of the same feather – were not acting in good faith. There are limits to stupidity or to candour. Among doctors we do not talk of disease and of curing disease the way we do to our patients. And when it is a question of a man's honour, of a man's liberty – personally I didn't give a damn since I was pleading guilty, often against them – but, as I say, when it is a question of a man's honour, one doesn't mouth moral platitudes for Sunday schools.

And my crime? After an hour of arguments I had already understood that it was and would remain relegated to second place, that as little would be said about it as possible. My crime was embarrassing – shocking –

and did not belong to the category of things that could happen to you, that threaten you. This feeling was so evident that I should not have been surprised to hear one of the gentlemen declare:

'She got what she deserved!'

But my 'concubine under the conjugal roof', and that Christmas Eve, so calm and so austere, so happy ... Yes, your Honour, so happy. Armande, who still suspected nothing, spent the evening teasing Frachon, who is her regularly appointed butt and who revels in his role. I played and chattered with my daughters for a long time while Mama told Martine all about our life at Ormois – and on this subject she is inexhaustible.

We all kissed one another at midnight and, before that, I had gone to the dining-room to light the candles on the tree and to put the chilled champagne on the table. I kissed Martine last. Isn't it a night when one has a right to kiss everybody? And I did it chastely, I assure you, without any improper insistence.

Now, why, when it was time to go to bed, shouldn't my wife have gone upstairs by herself and let me go home with Martine, instead of asking Frachon to take her?

Don't protest, you Honour. I haven't finished, and this is a question I've wanted for a long time to examine fully. I asked why, and I'm going to explain the reason for my question. At that period it had been months, I might say years, since Armande and I had had sexual relations. For during the last few years if it happened once in a long time it was only by some unexpected accident, so unexpected that afterwards Armande was embarrassed.

This sexual question was never discussed between us.

It had been none the less plain to both of us from the beginning of our marriage that we were not attracted to each other physically.

She put up with this semi-chastity, that's true. As for me, although I occasionally indulged in banal distractions outside, I haven't mentioned them, because they were too trifling to mention. I wanted them to be trifling because I was brought up to respect what exists, what is – to respect a thing, not because it is respectable, but because it is.

After all, it is in the name of this principle that they too, all the gentlemen of the law, discoursed.

And my house *was*, my family *was,* and to safeguard them both I restricted myself for years to living the life of an automaton instead of that of a man, until sometimes I felt like sinking down on the nearest bench and never getting up again.'

On the witness-stand Armande said, and this time you were present, for I noticed you in the crowd:

'I have given him ten years of my life, and, should he be free tomorrow, I am ready to give him the rest.'

No, your Honour, no! Why can't people be honest? Or think before they pronounce phrases like that which start a little shiver of admiration running through an audience?

Note that today I am convinced Armande did not speak in that way to make an impression on the judges, or on the public, or on the press. It has taken me a long time to come to this conclusion, but now I am willing to admit her sincerity.

And that is what is so terrifying: that there can exist for years between two people living together such irremediable misunderstandings.

In what way, will you tell, in what way did she *give me ten years of her life*? Where are they, those ten years? What have I done with them? Where have I put them? Forgive this bitter jesting. Those ten years, all joking apart, she lived them herself and you can't deny it. She came into my house to live them and, what's more, to live them in her own way. I didn't force her to. I didn't deceive her as to the fate that awaited her.

It isn't my fault if our customs or laws provide that when a man and a woman enter a house to live together, even if they're only eighteen years old, they solemnly engage to live in exactly the same way until they die.

During those ten years, not only did she live her own life, but she imposed it on all the rest of us. Moreover, had it been otherwise, had we been on an equal footing, I could still have answered her:

'Granted that you gave me ten years of your life, I also gave you ten years of mine. We're quits.'

Perhaps she did not always do what she wanted to during those ten years. Didn't she devote herself to the care of my daughters? Didn't she nurse me during a short illness? Didn't she give up trips she would like to have taken?

So did I.

And because I had no taste for her flesh, I renounced, so to speak, the flesh. I would sometimes wait weeks before going to rid myself of my sexual preoccupation with God knows whom, on the sly, under conditions that make me blush today.

I reached the point where I envied people who had some hobby as a safety valve – billiards, for example, cards, prize fights, or football. Such people know at least that they belong to a sort of fraternity and, thanks to that, ridiculous though it may appear, they never feel altogether isolated or abandoned in the world.

She said: 'When he introduced the young woman into my house, I did not know that . . .'

Her house. You too heard her. She did not say *our* house. She said *my* house.

Her house, her maid, her husband . . .

There you have the key to the enigma, your Honour, for enigma there must be since nobody understood or seemed to understand. She never went so far as to talk about *her* patients, but she used to say *our* patients and would question me about them, on the treatment I had prescribed, give me her advice – often very much to the point, I must say – as to the surgeon to whom they should be sent for an operation.

Incidentally – I just spoke of belonging to a fraternity. Well, there is one and only one to which I belong by the force of circumstances and that is the medical profession. But because all the doctors in our circle were our friends, though more Armande's friends than mine, I never had that feeling of solidarity which would at times have fortified me.

I am sure she always thought that she was acting for the best. Knowing her as I do now, I think it would be a terrible disillusionment if she ever perceived that her conduct had not always been practically faultless.

She was convinced, like the judges, like everybody at the trial, that I am a coward, that it was through cowardice that I organized that Christmas Eve, the memory of which was so painful to her, and through cowardice that I schemed – let's say the word – to get Martine into my home.

My home, you understand? I insist on that. Because,

after all, it seems to me that it was my home too, wasn't it?

And I did scheme, it is true. Only I should hardly be reproached for that since I was the one who suffered the most from it, I was the most humiliated by it.

Not only I, but Martine. Martine even more than I.

By inference, during the trial, they treated her as an adventuress, which was most convenient. They did not dare come out with the word itself because then, in spite of my two guards, I would have leaped out of the prisoner's dock. But, it seemed no less clear to everyone that she had wormed her way into our family for her own advantage.

A girl, it was true, who came from a good family – the gentlemen of the law never fail to salute the family, as at the cemetery, because among people of the same world certain civilities are due – a girl from a good family, but a black sheep who for four years had worked here, there and everywhere, and had slept with men.

I don't say who had had lovers. She had none before me. I say slept with men, just as I had slept with women.

But that's not the question now, and in addition it is nobody's business but mine.

She came from God knows where, she arrived in our honest town, with her poor little tailored suit that wasn't warm enough, her two suitcases, and her anaemic complexion, and, behold, she insinuates herself shamelessly into a well-heated, well-lighted house with substantial bourgeois meals, and from one day to the next becomes a doctor's assistant and almost the friend of his wife, who even goes out of her way to buy her a Christmas present.

It is terrifying to think that we are all human beings, all of us forced to bend our backs, more or less, under an unknown sky, and that we refuse to make the least little effort to understand one another.

But for her to enter our home like that, your Honour, by the back door, as it were – to enter our home thanks to a whole tangled web of lies imposed upon her by me, was not only the worst humiliation but the sacrifice of everything that she could still consider her personality.

If she had gone to work for Raoul Boquet, for instance. Suppose she had become his mistress, which is what would probably have happened. The whole town would have know about it, for the director of the Galleries does not suffer from an excess of delicacy. She would at once have become one of the little group at the Poker-Bar. She would have made friends there, men and women living like her, smoking and drinking like her, helping her to look upon her existence as normal.

The Poker-Bar? Even I, your Honour, before knowing Martine, would sometimes find myself looking wistfully at those creamy lights and longing to become one of the pillars of the place.

To have a round of lights where one could take refuge, you understand? Take refuge while still remaining one-self, among people who let you think you are someone.

In my house she was nothing. For three weeks she lived in constant terror of a suspicious glance from Armande, and this obsession became so strong that I was obliged to treat her nerves.

Even in the matter of work she was denied the simple self-satisfaction which is the right of the meanest labour-er. She was an excellent secretary before knowing me. On the other hand, she was totally ignorant of the medical profession, and I had no time to teach her. That wasn't why I wanted her near me.

I have seen her for days on end in a corner of my office, poring over old files which she had to pretend to be classifying.

Now that Martine was in our employ, whenever Armande spoke to her it was usually to ask her to telephone the dressmaker or one of the tradesmen.

We had to hide, it's true. And we often lied.

Through mercy, your Honour!

Because at that time I was still naïve, because at forty I knew nothing of love and because I imagined that at last I could be happy without taking away anything from others.

It seemed to me that with a little goodwill it would be so easy to arrange matters! We, Martine and I, were doing our part for the very reason that we consented to hide and to lie. Wouldn't it have been logical to expect others to make an effort too?

Was it my fault if I needed, as much as I needed air to breathe, this woman whom, two weeks ago, I'd not even heard of and whom I had not tried to know?

If a sudden illness had put my life in danger, the greatest specialists would have been called in, all the established order and ways of the household would have been disrupted, every one would have sacrificed himself, I would have been sent to Switzerland or somewhere else, they might have pushed duty – or pity – to the point of taking me out in a wheel chair.

Something different, but just as grave, had happened to me. My life was equally at stake. I am not being romantic. I speak of what I know for a fact, your Honour. For weeks I spent my nights without her. For weeks she would return to her apartment at meal-times. And besides, every day I had my round of visits to make.

For weeks, a dozen times, by day and by night, I would feel that lacerating sensation of emptiness I have already mentioned, so that I would have to remain stock still, my hand on my heart, panic in my eyes, like a cardiac. And do you think I could stand it without interruption, without hope, day after day, from morning to night and from night to morning?

What right had they to demand it of me, will you tell me? Don't begin talking of my daughters. That argument is too easy. Children don't enter into such questions at all, and among my patients I have seen enough ill-assorted or discordant couples to know that, except in popular fiction, children do not suffer in the least.

And my mother? Well, let's just crudely admit that mamas are not always saints, and that mine was jubilant at the idea that at last there was someone on this earth to shake off, if only secretly, the yoke of her daughter-in-law.

There remains Armande and her ten years. I know.

Now, let's put the question differently. I loved someone else. That was a fact. It was too late to retrace my steps. I was no longer able to get that love out of my system.

Even supposing that I once loved Armande, I did not love her any longer.

That is another fact. That's plain, isn't it?

So the blow, if blow there was, had already fallen. For, after all, when one loves a person the pain comes first from not being loved and then from knowing that the person one loves loves another.

All that, your Honour, had already happened.

Note that, for the moment, I accept the extreme hypothesis, that I concede for the sake of argument that

Armande had really loved me in every sense of the word and still loved me.

In that case, her attitude to my mind, on my soul and honour, becomes one of incredible ferocity. Always, of course, in the name of love.

'You don't love me any longer. You love someone else. Her presence is necessary to you. Nevertheless, because I still love you, I insist that you give her up and that you stay with me.'

To continue to live with someone you no longer love and who inflicts on you the most atrocious suffering, can you understand that? Think of evenings alone together beside the lamp, not forgetting the moment when these two people I'm talking about slip into bed and wish each other good night!

And yet, as I write these words, because of certain images they evoke for me, I have just conceded it. But on the condition that I accept Armande's love as an incontrovertible fact, a total love equal to mine for Martine.

But I do not believe that. A woman who loves does not say:

'. . . in my house . . . under my roof . . .'

A woman who truly loves does not speak of sacrificing ten years of her life.

She may have thought she loved me, your Honour, but I, you see, I know what love is.

Could she, had it been so, have said to me:

'If only you had been satisfied to see her outside . . .'

Would she have spoken of humiliation?

I swear to you, your Honour, that I am studying the question honestly, painfully, and strange as it may seem, it is especially since I am here that I study it without bias.

Because now other questions so much more important

have been answered, because I am far, very far, from all those bridling or gesticulating little men.

Isn't it true, my own Martine, isn't it true that we have gone a long way, both of us, that we have travelled, almost always thigh to thigh, the longest of all roads, the road where at the end one at last finds deliverance?

God knows that we embarked on that road without knowing it, innocently, yes, your Honour, like children, for we still were children.

We had no idea where we were going, but we could go in no other direction, and I remember, Martine, that, on certain days, just when we felt happiest, you would suddenly look at me with your eyes full of fear.

You were no more lucid than I, but life had dealt with you more roughly. Youth and its childish nightmares were closer to you and those nightmares still pursued you, even in my arms. How many times at night have you cried out, your forehead covered with sweat, clinging to my shoulder as though it alone could keep you from sliding down into the void, and I remember your voice on certain nights when your terror was at its height, as you kept repeating:

'Wake me, Charles. Quick! Wake me . . .'

Forgive me, Martine, for devoting as much attention to others as to you, but, you see, it is for you that I force myself to do it. You yourself used to murmur with regret:

'No one will ever know . . .'

And it is for her, your Honour, so that someone, so that one man will know, that I am writing all this to you.

Will you admit now that for me there is no question of lying, nor of disguising the truth the least bit in the world? At the point I have reached – we have reached, Martine and I – for we are together, your Honour –

one no longer lies. And if you cannot always follow my thought, cannot understand certain ideas which shock you, don't say to yourself that I am mad; think simply, humbly, that I have cleared a wall which perhaps you will one day clear yourself, on the other side of which one sees things differently.

Writing this, I am thinking of your telephone calls, of the anxious look you sometimes turned on me, waiting for my reply to certain questions. I think, above all, of other questions you were itching to ask me and which you never asked.

I said very little about Martine in your office. Because there are subjects one doesn't mention before a Maître Gabriel or before a poor honest fellow like your clerk.

I didn't speak of her at all at the trial, and that was variously interpreted. I couldn't very well say to them:

'But can't you understand that I delivered her . . .'

I couldn't shout these words that are truer still, words which rose in my throat, lacerated my throat:

'It was not she whom I killed. It was the other . . .'

Not counting that I would have been playing into their hands, giving them what they were trying to obtain for their peace of mind, even more than for their consciences' sake, for the honour of the whole bourgeois world to which they belonged, all of them.

Like a shot, and with both hands, my colleagues would have signed that certificate of insanity which, even at this late date, they are still bending all their efforts to justify, for it would settle so many things.

We didn't know, Martine and I, where we were going, and for weeks, out of pity, not to hurt anyone, and also because we did not yet know the all-devouring force of our love and its demands, we lived two lives, or more exactly, we lived a hallucinated existence.

I watched her arrive in the morning at eight o'clock in the raw January cold. I would be taking my breakfast in the kitchen while Armande was lingering upstairs.

Martine was not well at this time. She was paying. She was paying for many things. She was paying without complaining, without a thought of injustice. As she came through the gate and her feet crunched along the gravel walk, her eyes sought the kitchen window, knowing I was there, and she would smile without seeing me, a little uncertainly because someone might be observing her from a window upstairs, smile vaguely, tenderly at a curtain.

She never entered by the front door but by the door of the waiting-room. That was Armande's arrangement. I don't know the reason, I'd rather not know it. I never protested. She was to have the air of an employee since that was her status in our house. I am not blaming anyone, I assure you.

Did Babette notice our little stratagem? I never worried about it. I would swallow the rest of my coffee, go round through the front hall into my office, where she had had time to put on her white coat, and for a moment we would just stand looking at each other before falling into each other's arms.

We didn't dare speak, your Honour. Our eyes alone had that right. Don't think I have a mania of persecution. My mother was in the habit of creeping silently about the house and one was always bumping into her in places where one least expected to find her.

With Armande, it was not, I think, a mania, but a principle. Or better still, a right which she exercised without shame, the right of the mistress of the house to know everything that happened under her roof. The many times I have caught her listening behind a door she never blushed or showed the slightest embarrassment. No more than if I had come upon her giving orders to the maid or paying a tradesman's bill.

It was her right, her duty. No use dwelling on it. We accepted that too. Like hurrying to open the door for the first patient, because it has always squeaked a little and could, with a little attention, be heard from upstairs.

Throughout the morning the most we could expect were a few stolen glances, or the touch of her finger which I would brush with my hand when she held out the telephone to me, helped me take out some stitches, wash a wound, or hold a child still.

You are familiar with criminals but not with patients. If it is hard to make the former talk, it is equally hard to keep the latter from talking, and you can't imagine what it is like to see them file in, one after the other, for hours, all of them obsessed by their particular case, their aches and pains, their heart, their urine, their stools. And there we were, the two of us, only a step or two away from each other, everlastingly listening to the same complaints, while we ourselves had so many essential truths to tell each other.

If I were asked today how one can recognize love, if I had to make a diagnostic of love, I should say:

'First of all the need of nearness.'

I say advisedly a need as necessary, as absolute, as vital as a physical need.

'After that, the thirst to explain.'

A thirst to explain oneself, to explain the other, for, you see, one is so filled with wonder, or so conscious of a miracle, one is so afraid of losing this thing which one had never hoped for, which fate did not owe you and perhaps gave to you in a moment of distraction, that at every hour of the day one feels the need of being reassured and, in order to be reassured, of understanding.

A phrase spoken yesterday just before leaving, in Mme Debeurre's house. All night I am haunted by it. For hours on end I have turned it over and over in my mind to extract its quintessence. I have suddenly had the impression that it opened new horizons, threw new light on the two of us, on our incredible adventure.

And in the morning there was Martine. But instead of being able to compare my thoughts with hers at once I would be forced to live for hours in uncertainty, in agony.

This did not escape her. She would find a way of whispering between the patients or behind a patient's back.

'Is something wrong?'

And in spite of her anxious glance I would answer out of the corner of my mouth:

'Nothing . . . Later . . .'

We were devoured by the same impatience and the glances we exchanged over the heads of the patients were charged with questions.

'In just one word . . .'

Just one word to give her some inkling, because she was afraid, because we spent our whole time being afraid, of ourselves and of others. But how express such things in a word?

'It's nothing serious, I assure you . . .'

All right! Bring in the next one, a cyst or a sore throat, a boil or measles. That's all that counts, isn't it?

All the hours of the day, from one end to the other, would not have been enough, and yet everyone was bent on stealing from us even our tiniest crumbs of time, until, when finally, by force of scheming and lying, we were alone together, when I would arrive at her apartment after inventing God knows what to explain my going out in the evening, we were so hungry for one another that we found nothing more to say.

The great problem, the principal problem, was to discover why we loved each other, and it kept haunting us for a long time, for on its solution depended just how much confidence we could have in our love.

Did we find it, that solution?

I don't know, your Honour. No one will ever know. But why, ever since that first night at Nantes, after the first few hours which I freely qualify as sordid, when there was nothing to draw us together, why did we feel that sudden hunger for each other?

To begin with, you see, there was that rigid body, that open mouth, those distracted eyes which for me were first a mystery, then a revelation.

I had detested this little bar habitué, all her mannerisms and her assurance, and that come-hither look in the glances she cast at every man.

But when I held her in my arms that night, when, intrigued by what I did not understand, I suddenly turned on the light, I saw that I was embracing a little girl.

A little girl with a scar, it is true, from the pelvis to the navel, a little girl who had slept with men. I could even tell you now exactly how many men, and just how it occurred, under what circumstances, in what surroundings. A little girl, just the same, who was hungry for life and at the same time, to use one of my mother's expressions, scared blue of life.

Of life? Of her own, at any rate – afraid of herself, of

what she thought was herself, and I assure you she judged herself with terrible humility.

Even as a tiny little girl she was afraid, thought of herself as differently made from others, as not up to others, and that was why, you see, little by little, she invented a personality in the image of girls in magazines and novels.

To be like other people. To reassure herself.

As I, your Honour, might have taken up billiards or belote.

Including the cigarettes, the bars, the high stools and the crossed legs, including that aggressive familiarity with the barmen, that flirtatiousness with men, no matter what men.

'I'm not such a mess, after all . . .'

That was her expression in the beginning. She would repeat it everlastingly, she would keep asking at the slightest provocation:

'Am I really such a mess as all that?'

Not to feel a mess in her native city of Liège, where her parents' fortune was not such as to give her a sense of equality with the other girls she knew, she left home alone, put up a brave front, and succeeded in finding a small job in Paris.

Not to feel a mess, she began smoking and drinking. And, in another domain, more difficult to discuss, even in this letter which is for you alone, your Honour, she felt herself a mess.

When she was still a little girl, not more than ten years old, invited by little girls richer than herself whom her parents were very proud to have her visit, she would be a witness of their games which were not always entirely innocent.

I said girls richer than herself and I repeat it. Families whom she heard her parents speak of with admiration not exempt from envy, and also with the respect that in certain classes of society is paid to the classes above them. And when she wept, without knowing why, when she refused the following week to go back to their homes, she was treated as a big ninny and was forced to bow to parental authority.

All that is absolutely true, your Honour. There is an accent of truth that is unmistakable. But I was not satisfied with that truth. I went to see for myself. There is nothing related to her that I did not persist in knowing, including the most casual surroundings in which she had lived.

I went to Liège. I saw the convent of the Daughters of the Cross, where she had been one of the boarders in a blue pleated skirt, and a round hat with a broad brim. I saw her classroom, her desk and, still hanging on the wall and signed in her childish hand, some of the complicated pieces of embroidery that little girls are taught to make.

I saw her exercise books, I read her compositions, I know by heart the comments written by her teachers in red ink. I saw photographs of her at every age, photographs of commencements at school with the other pupils whose names I knew, photographs of the family in the country – uncles, aunts and cousins, who became more familiar to me than my own family.

What was it gave me the desire, what was it created in me the need of knowing all this, whereas, for example, I had never had the least curiosity about things connected with Armande?

I think, your Honour, it was the discovery I made of

her true personality. Call it intuition, if you like. And what I discovered was almost in spite of her, because, you see, she was ashamed of it.

I worked for weeks, and I mean literally worked, to deliver her from shame. And to do that I was forced to pry into the darkest corners.

At the beginning she lied. She lied like a little girl who tells her friends stories about the maid in her house, when her family has no maid.

She lied, and patiently I would untangle all the lies. I would force her to admit them one after the other. I had a complicated skein to unravel, but I held the end of the thread and never let go of it.

Because of her rich and depraved little friends, because of her own parents who persisted in sending her to play with them (their families being the most considerable in the city), she got into the habit, certain evenings, of stretching out on her stomach in the solitude of her bed, and of lying there rigid for hours straining fiercely for a spasm that never came.

Physiologically she was precocious, since at eleven she was a woman. For years she continued this desperate search for an impossible relief and that mouth, open as when I saw her at Nantes, your Honour, those eyes rolled back in her head, that pulse at a hundred and forty – these were her heritage from the little girl.

Men had merely taken the place of that solitary rigidity. And it was still for the sake of being like other people, of feeling like other people at last, that she had sought them.

Twenty-two. For at twenty-two she was still a virgin. She was still hoping.

What was she hoping for? Just what we have been

taught, what she had been taught to hope for – marriage, children, a peaceful house, everything that people call happiness. But in Paris, far from home, she was a little girl from a good family, without money.

And then one day, your Honour, a day of lassitude, of uneasiness, the little girl wanted to do what the others were doing, make sure she was made like the others. Without love, without poetry true or false, without any real desire! And for my part, I find that tragic.

With a stranger, with a body she did not know against her own, she began again the same attempts as the little girl in her solitary bed and because with all her might she wanted to succeed, because her whole being was straining for relief, the man was convinced that she was a passionate lover.

The others too, your Honour, who followed in succession – not one of them – not one, I tell you – understood that what she was looking for in their arms was a sort of deliverance. Not one suspected that she left their embrace with the same bitterness, the same nausea she had felt after her solitary experiments.

Is it because I was the first to have this revelation that I loved her and that she loved me?

Many other things, one after the other, I understood later on. It was like a rosary one tells slowly, bead by bead.

That round of warm light which is the common need of all of us, where is it to be found when one lives alone in a big city?

She discovered bars. She discovered cocktails. And for a few hours drink gave her that self-confidence she so much needed. And the men she met in such places were ready to help her believe in herself.

Didn't I confess that I might have become a pillar of the Poker-Bar, that I felt the temptation? I too would have found that easy appreciation I failed to find at home; I too would have found women who would have given me the illusion of love.

But she was humbler than I, in fact. I could still manage to withdraw into my shell, while she could not.

And a few drinks, your Honour, a few compliments, a vague semblance of admiration and tenderness would sweep away the last shreds of her resistance.

Haven't we all done the same thing, you and I, every man, even the most intelligent and the most virtuous? Haven't we all, at one time or another, sought in the vilest places, in the most mercenary caresses, a little solace, a little self-confidence?

She went with strangers, or practically. She went with them into hotel rooms. Men pawed her in their cars, in taxis.

As I told you, I have counted them. I know exactly every one of their gestures.

Do you see why it was that we had such an imperious need to talk to each other and that all the empty hours, the hours that were stolen from us, were torture?

Not only did she fail to find the desired relief, not only did she look in vain for that confidence in herself which would have restored to her a semblance of equilibrium, but she retained enough clear-headedness to be conscious of her progressive degradation.

When she came to La Roche, your Honour, when I met her at Nantes in the rain on the platform of a station after we had both missed our train, she was at the end of her resistance, she had given up the struggle, she was resigned to anything, including disgust for herself.

She was like – forgive the blasphemy, Martine, but you do understand – she was like a woman who, to feel secure at last, enters a brothel.

The miracle is that I met her, that double tardiness which brought us face to face. The miracle is, above all else, that I, who am not particularly intelligent, who have never, like certain of my colleagues, spent much time over problems of this kind – that I, Charles Alavoine, in the course of a night when I was drunk, when she too was drunk, and during which we had dragged our disgust through all the sordid rain-drenched streets of Nantes, suddenly understood.

Not even understood. I didn't understand at once. To be exact, let's say that I glimpsed, through all the darkness in which we were struggling, a tiny far-off ray of light.

The true miracle is, after all, that I had the desire to understand, God knows why – perhaps because I, too, felt alone, because I had sometimes longed to sink down on a bench and never to get up again, perhaps because there was still that little glow-worm, because everything had not gone out in me – the real miracle is that I wanted to draw nearer to that fraternal light and understand, and that this desire, of which I was not conscious, was enough to make me overcome all obstacles.

I didn't even know then that it was love.

Chapter Nine

A little while ago they came for my cell-mate to take him to the visitors' waiting-room. He is the one I told you about who looks like a young bull. For a long time I didn't know or care what his name was. It is Antoine Belhomme, I've since found out, and he was born in the Loiret.

I finally learned why he was so grim, his mouth bitter, his eyes sullen. They'd played him for a sucker, your Honour, to use his own expression. The fact was they didn't have sufficient evidence against him to take him before a jury. He didn't know this. He thought he was done for, and if he kept on denying his guilt it was only on principle, not to knuckle under. And that was when his examining magistrate, one of your colleagues, proposed a kind of bargain.

I suppose it wasn't discussed in any such frank terms. But I believe what Belhomme told me. They began by talking to him about the penitentiary and the guillotine. They had the young animal so terrified that cold sweat stood out on his forehead. Then the magistrate, when he thought him sufficiently softened up, gently hinted at the possibility of a compromise.

If he would confess, that would be taken into account, premeditation would be officially ruled out, since the murder weapon was a bottle he had picked up off the bar. His conduct during the preliminary hearings, as well as his good behaviour at the trial, would also be taken into consideration, and they promised him, at least they let him hope, that he would get off with not more than ten years.

He fell for it. He was so confident that, when he used to see his lawyer sweating blood trying to defend him, he himself would reassure him:

'Take it easy. I tell you it's in the bag.'

Just the same they double-crossed him. They slapped him with twenty years, the maximum ... All because, between the preliminary hearings and the trial, chance would have it that two other crimes of the same nature were committed in the outskirts of the city, and as a final stroke of bad luck, both of them by boys about his own age, giving rise to a furious press campaign. The papers talked of a wave of terror, a grave social danger, the necessity for drastic measures.

And my young bull was the goat. Forgive me if I am beginning to talk like him. At any rate, there's someone to whom it would be just as well not to make speeches about Society with a capital S, or Justice! You stink in his nostrils, the whole lot of you.

This is the first time he's had a visitor since we've been living together. He left like a meteorite, head first.

When he returned a moment ago, he was another man. His eyes shone with a pride I have rarely seen before.

'It was the girl . . .' he flung at me, not able to find other words. But he understood what he meant and so did I.

I knew that he was living with a girl barely fifteen years old who worked in a radio factory near the Puteaux Bridge. He had something else to tell me, but it was seething with such force in his throat, it was surging up from such depths that the words failed to come out right away:

'She's going to have a baby!'

As a doctor, your Honour, how many times have I been the first to announce this news to a young woman, often in the presence of her husband. I know all the various reactions of all kinds of people.

But such total happiness, a pride like that, I have never seen before. And he added simply:

'Now, as she says, she won't have to worry!'

Don't ask me why I have told you this story. I have

no idea. I'm not trying to prove anything. It has nothing in common with ours. And yet, perhaps, it might serve to explain what I mean by absolute love, and even what I mean by purity.

What purer, tell me, than this child, so proud, so happy to be coming to announce to her lover condemned to twenty years hard labour that she is going to have a child by him?

'*Now, I won't have to worry!*'

And *he* did not look worried when he came back to his cell.

In a certain sense there was something of the same purity in our love. It was just as total, if this word can make you understand how we accepted it beforehand, without our understanding it, without knowing just what was happening to us, with no idea of the extreme consequences.

It is because Martine loved me like that that I loved her. It is perhaps because I loved her with the same innocence – you may smile if you like – that she gave me her love.

A vicious circle? I can't help it. We here enter into a domain, your Honour, where it is difficult to explain what one means, especially to those who do not know.

How much simpler it would be to tell our story to Antoine Belhomme, who would need no commentaries.

Before the thing happened, in my wife's house, as I willingly call it from now on, we had already, Martine and I, learned to know suffering.

I wanted to find out everything about her (I have already told you that) and, docilely, after a few attempts at lying – for she was trying not to hurt me – she told me everything, she even told me too much, feeling so culpable she even overcharged herself with sins, as I perceived later on.

Her arrival at La Roche-sur-Yon, in that rainy December, after a detour by way of Nantes to borrow a little money, was after all a sort of suicide. She had given up. When one reaches a certain degree of disgust for oneself, one degrades oneself even further so as to reach the end, the bottom, more quickly, because after that nothing worse can happen to one.

But, instead of that, a man offered her life.

In doing so I took on, and I fully realized it, a heavy responsibility. I felt that she had to be delivered from herself, from her past, from those few years, those very few years in which she had lost everything.

And that past, I thought, in order to accomplish this, I would have to take in hand myself.

I receive many of the journals on psycho-analysis. And although I have not always read them, I do know something about the subject. Certain of my colleagues in the provinces have taken it up, and have always terrified me.

Wasn't it necessary that I should purge her of her memories? I sincerely believed it. I have not, I think, the least predisposition to sadism or to masochism.

If not to deliver her, why should I have spent hours on end confessing her, relentlessly poking into all the most sordid, the most humiliating corners?

I was jealous, your Honour, ferociously jealous. I am going to confess a ridiculous detail on this subject. When I met Raoul Boquet a little later on, about the fifteenth of January, I wouldn't greet him. I frankly stared at him without bowing.

Because he had known her before me! Because he had

offered her a drink and she had accepted. Because he had known the other Martine.

The Martine *before* me, the Martine I hated, whom I had hated at first sight and whom she herself also hated.

I did not create the new Martine. I have no such pretension. I don't take myself for God the Father. The new Martine, you see, was the oldest; it was the little girl of the past who had never ceased to exist altogether, and my sole merit, if merit there is, was to have discovered her under a litter of false pretences of which she was the first dupe.

I undertook at all costs to restore her confidence in herself, her confidence in life, and it was with this end in view that, together, with dogged perseverance, we ventured upon the great cleansing.

When I say that I know everything about her past, be assured that I mean literally everything, including those gestures, thoughts, reactions which one human being so rarely confides to another.

I have known appalling nights. But the bad Martine was gradually disappearing and that was all that mattered. I watched another Martine being born little by little, one who every day grew more and more to resemble a snapshot she had given me, taken when she was sixteen.

I no longer fear ridicule. Here, one no longer fears anything except oneself. Every human being, even if his whole fortune consists of only two suitcases, drags around with him through the years a certain number of objects.

We sort them all out. A sorting so implacable, with such a determination to kill certain things once and for all, that a pair of shoes, for instance – I can still see them, they were almost new – which she had worn one evening when she had picked up a strange man, were burned in the fireplace.

Practically nothing remained of the clothes she had brought with her and I, who could never spend my money without first going to Armande, was unable to replace them.

Her suitcases were empty, her wardrobe reduced to the bare necessities.

It was January. Think of the wind, the cold, the short days, the shadows and the lights of the little city, of the two of us struggling to extricate our love from everything that threatened to stifle it. Think of my office-hours, of the anguish of our separations, and finally of Mme Debeurre's little house, which was our only haven, and to which I came panting with emotion.

Think of all the agonizing problems we had to solve, of the other problems presented by our life in Armande's house and still further complicated by our constant solicitude for her peace of mind.

Of course we lied. And it is gratitude we deserve, if not admiration, for we had something better to do than to worry about other people's tranquillity.

We had to discover each other. We had to get used to living with our love, we had to – if I may be allowed the word – transplant our love into our daily life and domesticate it.

And I saw thirty patients every morning! And I lunched without Martine, between Mama and Armande, opposite my daughters! I talked with them. I must have succeeded in talking to them like an ordinary person, since Armande – the subtle, the intelligent Armande – saw nothing.

Duplicity, you say, your Honour? Good heavens! Do

you know that sometimes, when I was at table with my family – that's right, with my family, and Martine wasn't there! – suddenly there, on the retina of my eye, would be the image of a man and the brutal memory of a gesture she had made, as distinct as a pornographic photograph.

Your Honour, I don't wish anybody anything like that! The pain of absence is horrible, but that is one pain which makes you believe in hell.

Yet I still sat there, and I suppose I ate. They told me of all the little happenings of the day and I replied.

I had to see her at once – that, for God's sake, you must understand! – to be sure that a new Martine really existed, that she was not the one in the obscene photograph. I watched for her. I counted the minutes, the seconds. She opened the gate, I heard her footsteps on the gravel path, she was walking towards the house with that uncertain smile which she always offered me in advance in case I stood in need of reassurance.

Once when she came into my office I stared at her without seeing her. The Other had remained glued to my retina and suddenly, in spite of myself, *for the first time in my life,* I struck someone.

I couldn't stand it any longer. I couldn't stand the pain. I was at the end of my endurance. I did not strike with my open hand, but with my fist, and I felt the impact of bone against bone.

Immediately afterwards I collapsed. The reaction. I fell on my knees, I'm not ashamed to admit it. And she, your Honour, she smiled, looking at me tenderly through her tears.

She was not crying. There were tears in her eyes, the tears of a little girl who has been deeply hurt, but she did not cry. She smiled, and I assure you that, though sad, she was happy.

She stroked my forehead, my hair, my eyes, my cheeks, my mouth. She murmured:

'My poor Charles . . .'

I thought it would never happen again, that never again would the beast be aroused in me. I loved her, your Honour, I'd like to shout that word till I'm hoarse.

Yet, I did it again. Once, at her place, *our* place, one evening when we were lying together in the bed, when I was caressing her, my fingers touched the scar and all my phantoms returned.

Because I had begun to love her body in an almost insane way that made her smile, but smile with a secret uneasiness beneath her amusement.

'It isn't Christian, Charles. It isn't right . . .'

I loved everything about her, her skin, her saliva, her sweat, and above all – oh, above all – her early morning face, which at that time I hardly ever saw, for it took the miracle of an urgent call to give me the chance to go to her early in the morning and to awaken her.

What Mme Debeurre thought of us, I don't give a damn. Does a thing like that count, when one is living an experience like ours?

Once when I wakened her like that, she was pale, with her hair spread out on the pillow, and in her sleep she wore a childlike expression that took my breath away, murmuring, her eyelids still closed:

'Papa . . .'

Because her father too loved her early morning face, because her father used to tiptoe over to her bed in those days, not so very long ago, when he was still alive and she was still a little girl.

She was not beautiful like that, your Honour. There was no resemblance to a cover girl, let me tell you, and I did not want her to be beautiful ever again with that sort of beauty. The red had disappeared from her lips, the black from her lashes, the powder from her cheeks, and she was just simply a woman again, and little by little she became for the whole day what she was early in the morning in her sleep.

Sometimes I was under the impression that I had gone over her face with an eraser. In the beginning she seemed indistinct, like a drawing half rubbed out. It was only gradually that her true face appeared, that the fusion with what she had been *before* was accomplished.

If you don't understand that, your Honour, it is useless for me to continue, but I have chosen you just because I felt that you would understand.

I haven't created anything. I have never had the presumption to try to fashion a woman in the image of woman as I conceived her.

It was Martine, the real Martine before the bastards had sullied her, that I persisted in trying to extricate. She was the one I loved and whom I love, who is mine, who is so much a part of my own body that I can no longer distinguish between them.

Mme Debeurre probably heard everything, our murmurs, my shouting, my rages, my blows. And what of it? Was it our fault?

Armande said later on:

'What must that woman have thought?'

No, really, your Honour, just weigh the evidence, I beg you! On the one hand my house – our house, Armande's house – with its armchairs, its red carpet on the stairs and its brass rods, the bridge parties and the dress-

maker, Mme Debeurre and her misfortunes – her husband killed by a train and her cyst, for she had a cyst –
and on the other, the exploration we had undertaken,
gambling everything we had in this game to the limit,
without mental reservations of any kind, at the risk of
our life.

Yes, at the risk of our life.

That, Martine understood before I did. She said
nothing then. It is the only thing she kept from me. And
that is why at certain moments she would look at me with
dilated pupils as if she didn't see me.

She was looking farther ahead, she was seeing another
me, the future me, as I saw in her the little Martine of
the past.

She did not draw back, your Honour. She did not hesitate an instant. And yet, if you only knew how afraid
she was of dying, a childish fear of everything connected
with death!

It was the day following a day when I had been bat-
tling with the past, with the other Martine and with my
phantoms – the day following a day when I had struck
her with even greater violence – that we were caught.

It was eight o'clock. My wife was, or should have
been, upstairs with my youngest daughter who was not
going to school that day. Patients were waiting in a line
on the benches in the waiting-room. I hadn't the heart
to open the door for them right away.

One of Martine's eyes was badly bruised. She smiled,
and her smile was all the more touching because of that.
I was overflowing with shame and tenderness. After my
fit of rage I had spent an almost sleepless night.

I took her in my arms. With infinite gentleness – I
mean it – with infinite gentleness. I was capable of that,

183

and I felt that I was both her father and her lover. I understood that from now on, no matter what happened, we were alone in the world, just the two of us, that her flesh was my flesh, that a day would come very soon when we would no longer need to question each other and when my phantoms would vanish.

I stammered in her ear, still cold with the cold of the street:

'Forgive me . . .'

I was not ashamed. I was no longer ashamed of my outbursts, my fits of violence, because I knew now that they were a part of our love, that our love, just as it was, just as we wanted it to be, could not have existed without them.

We didn't move. She leaned her head on my shoulder. At that moment, I remember, I was looking far away, both into the past and into the future. I was beginning to measure with terror the road that remained to be travelled.

I am not making this up after the event. It would be unworthy of me and of her. I had no premonition, I tell you that at once. Nothing but the vision of that road along which we walked alone.

I sought her lips to give me courage, and then the door to the front hall opened. We didn't jump apart, it didn't even occur to us, when we saw Armande standing in the doorway. We remained with our arms around each other. She looked at us and said – I can still hear the sound of her voice:

'Excuse me . . .'

Then she went out and the door slammed.

Martine did not understand why I started to smile, why my face showed a positive joy.

My feeling was one of relief. At last!

'Don't worry, darling. And don't cry. Please, don't cry.'

I didn't want any tears. None were needed. Someone knocked at the door. It was Babette.

'Mme Alavoine would like to see you, sir. She is in her bedroom.'

Of course, my good Babette! Of course, Armande! It was time. I couldn't stand any more. I was suffocating.

Be calm, Martine. I know that you are trembling, that the little girl you are expects another beating. Haven't you always been beaten?

Trust me, darling. I'm going upstairs. And the reason I'm going up there, you see, is to find freedom for our love.

There are words, your Honour, which never should be spoken, which size up one person while they liberate another.

'I suppose you'll send her packing now?'

No, Armande. Of course not. No question of that.

'In any case I will not allow her to remain another hour under my roof . . .'

Well, well, my lady, since it is your roof . . . pardon me. I am wrong. And all day long I was wrong. I spat out all my venom. Ah, yes, I spat it out for an hour without stopping, pacing up and down like a wild animal in a cage, between the bed and the door, while Armande, keeping a dignified attitude, stood by the window clutching the curtain with one hand.

I ask your pardon, too, Armande, surprising as it may seem to you. For it was all so useless, so superfluous.

I vomited all the rancour in my heart, all my humiliations, all my cowardice, my suppressed desires. I even

185

added to them, and the whole load I flung on to your shoulders, yours alone, as though henceforth you and you alone were to bear the full responsibility.

You, who have never been lacking in sang-froid, I saw you lose your poise and there was even an expression of fear in your eyes as you looked at me, because, in the man who had slept in your bed for ten years, you were discovering another man whose existence you had never suspected.

I yelled at you, and they must have heard me downstairs:

'I love her, do you understand? *I lo-ve her!*'

And then, baffled, you said to me:

'If only . . .'

I can't remember your exact words. I was feverish. The night before I had viciously struck another woman, another woman whom I loved.

'If only you had been satisfied with seeing her outside . . .'

I burst into a rage, your Honour. Not only against Armande. Against all of you, against life as you understand it, against the idea you have of the union of two beings and the heights of passion they can attain.

I was wrong. I regret it. She could not understand. She was no more responsible than the district attorney or Maître Gabriel.

Unsteadily she kept repeating:

'Your patients are waiting for you . . .'

And what about Martine! Wasn't Martine waiting for me?

'We'll discuss this later when you are calmer.'

Not at all. Right away, like an emergency operation.

'If you need her so much . . .'

186

Because, you see, I had blurted out the whole truth. Everything. Including Martine's bruised face, the work of my fists, and even my biting the sheets during my sleepless nights.

So then I was offered a compromise. I could go to see her, like a Boquet – I could, in fact, if I would be discreet about it, go, from time to time, to satisfy the demands of nature!

The house must have trembled. I became violent, brutal – I, whom my mother had always compared to a great gentle dog, even too gentle.

I was malicious, wilfully cruel. I needed to be. I couldn't have found relief otherwise.

'Think of your mother . . .'

'To hell with her.'

'Think of your daughters . . .'

'To hell with them.'

To hell with everything! It was over, all that, with one stroke, just when I least expected it, and I had no desire to begin all over again.

Babette knocked at the door. Babette announced timorously:

'Mademoiselle says you're wanted on the phone, sir.'

'I'm coming.'

It was Martine, Martine holding out the telephone without a word, resigned to the worst, Martine who had already given up.

'Hello! Who is speaking?'

A real case. A real 'emergency'.

'I'll be there in a few minutes.'

I turned and said:

'Tell the people who are waiting . . .'

In the most natural way in the world, your Honour.

For me, everything was settled. I saw how pale she was, standing there in front of me, her lips colourless. And I almost got angry.

I had already picked up my bag. I took down my coat which was hanging on the back of the door.

It never occurred to me to kiss her.

'We are leaving, both of us . . .'

It was that evening, about nine o'clock. I had chosen a night train on purpose, so that my daughters would be asleep. I went up to kiss them in their beds. I insisted on going alone. I stayed upstairs for several minutes, and only my elder daughter half opened her eyes.

I went down again, very calm. The taxi was waiting outside the gate and the driver was taking out my baggage.

Mama had stayed in the drawing-room. Her eyes were red, and her handkerchief was a little wet ball in her hand. I thought it would go off all right after all, but at the last moment, as I disengaged myself from her arms, she stammered before bursting into sobs:

'You are leaving me alone with her . . .'

Armande was standing in the front hall. It was she who had packed my bags. She continued to think of everything, sent Babette to look for a travelling-case which had been forgotten.

The light was on in the hall. We could hear Mama's muffled sobs and, outside, the purring of the motor the driver had started.

'Goodbye, Charles . . .'

'Goodbye, Armande . . .'

And then we both opened our mouths and spoke exactly the same words at the same moment:

'No hard feelings . . .'

We smiled in spite of ourselves. I took her in my arms and kissed her on both cheeks; she imprinted a kiss on my forehead. As she pushed me towards the door, she breathed:

'Go . . .'

I went to get Martine and once again we found ourselves together on a station platform. This time it was not raining and I have never seen so many stars in the sky. Poor Martine, who was frightened again, who asked me just as we were getting into our compartment:

'You're sure you won't regret it?'

We were alone. We turned out the lights immediately and I held her close, so close that we must have looked like one of those emigrant couples you see embracing on the steerage deck of ocean liners.

We too, we were leaving for the unknown.

What could we have said to each other that night? Even when I felt the warmth of a tear on my cheek, I did not try to find words to reassure her and was content simply to stroke her eyelids.

She finally fell asleep and I counted all the stations with their lights filing by on the other side of the curtain. At Tours some people, loaded down with baggage, opened our door. Their eyes peered into the darkness, saw our bodies lying in a close embrace.

They went away on tiptoe, after softly closing the door again.

This was not a flight, you know. Before leaving we had settled everything very decently, Armande and I. We even considered for hours certain details of our future.

More than that! Armande gave me her advice in a somewhat hesitating voice and with an air of apology.

Not advice with regard to Martine, naturally, but about my business.

What greatly facilitated the adjustment of our affairs was that, by a miracle, young Braille was available. He is a young doctor from a very poor family – his mother is a cleaning woman in the neighbourhood of the Austerlitz Station – who for lack of money could not hope to go into practice for himself for years.

In the meantime, he takes over other doctors' practices when he is needed. I knew him because he had been my substitute during my last vacation, and had done very well.

Armande having agreed, I telephoned him in Paris. Because of the winter sports, I was afraid he would have been engaged by some colleague who was going to spend a few weeks at Chamonix or Mégève.

He was free. He agreed to come at once and to take over my practice for an indeterminate period. I don't know if he understood. For my part, I tried to intimate that he could stay for ever if he wanted to.

He was given a room in the house, the one Martine had occupied for two nights. He is a young redhead, a little too tense, too impatient for my taste – you are too conscious that some day he intends to get even with life – but most people like him.

Thus, there is hardly any change in the house at La Roche. I left them the car. Armande, my mother and my daughters will be able to live on exactly the same scale as before; young Braille being satisfied with a fixed salary, there will be a large margin of profit.

'Don't take just anything that comes along,' Armande advised me, 'and don't accept the first price that is proposed . . .'

For I was, of course, to keep on with my work. I first thought of looking for a place in one of the large laboratories in Paris, but that would force me to leave Martine for a part of the day. I frankly admitted this to Armande and she murmered, with a smile which was not as ironic as I might have feared:

'You are as afraid as all that?'

I am jealous, but I am not afraid. It is not because I am afraid that I am unhappy, lost, on edge, as soon as I leave her for a moment.

What's the use of explaining that to Armande, who, moreover, I would swear, understood very well.

By drawing on only a part of our savings I could buy a practice in the Paris suburbs. The rest, almost everything we possess, I left for Armande and the children. I didn't even have to sign a power of attorney because I had given her one long ago. So that is how things were settled. And, I repeat, we were able to discuss it all calmly. Everything was slightly veiled, you understand? Instinctively we spoke in a low tone.

'Do you plan to come back to see your daughters from time to time?'

'I plan to come often . . .'

'Without her?'

I did not reply.

'You won't inflict that on me, Charles?'

I promised nothing.

We left, Martine and I, and we spent the night in each other's arms on the bench of the compartment, without saying a word.

The sun was shining over the Paris suburbs when we arrived. We stopped at a decent, commonplace hotel near the station, and I registered:

'M. and Mme Charles Alavoine...'

We were serving our apprenticeship in our new-found freedom and were still a little clumsy. A dozen times a day we would eye each other, and the one who was caught, if I can put it that way, would quickly smile.

Whole neighbourhoods in Paris frightened me because they were peopled with phantoms – that is, with flesh and blood men we were in danger of meeting.

And so, your Honour, as though by common consent, we avoided them. Sometimes, at a corner of a street or avenue, we would turn aside to the right or the left without having to say a word, and I would hasten to squeeze Martine's arm affectionately, feeling her lapse into sadness.

She was also afraid of seeing me depressed by the necessity of starting my career all over again, while I, on the contrary, was filled with joy. I was doing my best to begin from scratch.

We went together to the agencies which specialize in doctors' offices and we visited many such offices scattered all over the city, in poor neighbourhoods and in prosperous neighbourhoods.

Why was it that the poor neighbourhoods tempted me more than the others? I felt the need of getting away from a certain milieu which reminded me of my other life and it seemed that the more completely we could get away from it, the more completely Martine would be mine.

We finally fixed our choice, after only four days of hunting, on an office situated in Issy-les-Moulineaux, in the drabbest, the most teeming part of the working-class suburb.

My predecessor was a Roumanian who had made a

fortune and was going back to his own country. Naturally he exaggerated the merits of his office.

It was practically a factory and my office hours were more like an assembly line. The waiting-room, with whitewashed walls covered with scribblings, made one think of a public building. Patients smoked and spat. And there would certainly have been a fight if I had ever had the notion of taking any patient out of turn.

It was on the ground floor. It faced the street and you entered directly as into a shop, without a bell or a maid to answer it. You took your place at the end of the line and you waited.

My consulting-room, where we spent most of our day, Martine and I, opened on to a courtyard, and in this courtyard was a blacksmith who pounded iron from morning to night.

As for our apartment on the fourth floor, it was quite new but with such tiny rooms that it seemed like a doll's house. We had been obliged to take over the Roumanian's furniture, factory-made furniture, like the sets one sees in the windows of department stores.

I bought a little second-hand car, a five cylinder, since Issy-les-Moulineaux is as large as a provincial city and I had patients from one end of it to the other. Besides I admit that at the beginning what humiliated me most was having to wait interminable minutes for the tram at the corner.

Martine learned to drive and obtained her licence. She served as my chauffeur.

Was there any way in which she did not serve me? We had difficulty finding a regular maid. We were waiting for answers to the advertisements we had put in provincial newspapers and we got along meantime with a cleaning woman, as dirty as a pig and mean as hell, who consented to come in for two or three hours a day.

Nevertheless, Martine always came down with me at half-past seven for my office hours, donned her white coat and cap and got everything ready. We would go out for lunch together, generally to a little chauffeurs' restaurant, and sometimes she would lift anxious eyes to mine.

I had to keep repeating:

'But I swear, I am very happy . . .'

It was true, it was really life beginning again for me, almost from zero. I should have liked to be still poorer, to start from the very bottom.

Then she would drive me through the crowded streets, wait for me in front of my patient's house and in the evening, whenever it was possible, we would go marketing together so that we could have dinner in our toy apartment.

We went out very little. We had involuntarily adopted the habits of our neighbourhood: once a week in the evening we would go to the same films as my patients, a theatre that smelt of oranges, chocolate ice cream and synthetic fruit drops, and where you walked on peanut shells.

We made no plans for the future. Isn't that the proof that we were happy?

Chapter Ten

There wasn't a night, your Honour, that we fell asleep – her head nestled in the hollow of my shoulder, and often the next morning we would wake in the same position – as I say, there wasn't a night that we closed our eyes without my having permeated her flesh.

It was almost a solemn, a ritualistic act. For her, it was an agonizing moment, knowing as she did what a price I would pay, would make her pay, for the least reappearance of the Other. What had to be prevented at any cost was the sudden collapse of her nerves, that rigidity which was so painful to me, that desperate breathless tension towards a relief that never came and for which she used to struggle until strength failed her.

'You see, Charles, I'll never be like other women.'

I comforted her, but I often doubted it myself. And so it was that we often feared this act which separated our days from our nights and by which we sought to mingle our blood.

'Some day when you least expect it, you'll see, the miracle will happen . . .'

And the miracle did happen. I remember the astonishment I read in her eyes, in which apprehension still lingered. Feeling the thread still too tenuous, I did not yet dare risk a word of encouragement, and I pretended that I did not notice what was happening.

'Charles . . .'

I hugged her tighter in my arms and, at the same time,

more tenderly, and it was really a little girl's voice that asked:

'May I?'

She could, indeed. It was really her flesh this time that was quickened, my eyes could not leave her eyes. Then she uttered a great cry, a cry such as I have never heard, an animal cry and at the same time a cry of triumph. She smiled a new smile in which both pride and confusion mingled – for she was a little embarrassed – and, when her head fell back on the pillow, when her body limply relaxed, she stammered:

'At last!'

At last, yes, your Honour, at last she was mine in all plenitude. At last she was a woman. At last, too, besides her love, I possessed something the others had never had. They suspected nothing, they had never noticed, but what of it!

We had just passed an important stage. This victory, if I can put it that way, had to be consolidated; we had to make sure that it should not be merely an isolated accident.

Don't smile, if you would be so kind. Won't you try to understand? Don't act like the others who have pored over my case, like that Justice, one of whose servants you are, who refused to see what was really important in my crime.

It was a few nights later, just when we were at our happiest, just when she was falling asleep in my arms, saturated with my love, while my hand was unconsciously stroking her soft skin, that, almost without realizing it, I said to myself:

'And to think that I shall have to kill her one day.'

Those are exactly the words which formed in my brain.

I did not, to be sure, believe it, but neither was I horrified. I continued to caress her thigh in my favourite spot, her hair tickled my cheek, I felt her regular breath on my neck and I spelled out in the dark of my consciousness:

'I shall have to kill her . . .'

I was not asleep. I had not yet reached that state which is not altogether waking but is not sleep either, and in which one enjoys a terrifying clarity of mind.

I did not push her away. I kept on caressing her. She was dearer to me than ever. She was my whole life.

But at the same time, in spite of anything she could do, in spite of her love, her humble love – mind that word, your Honour, her love was humble – she was at the same time the Other, and she knew it.

We both knew it. We both suffered from the knowledge. We lived, acted, spoke as if the Other had never existed. Sometimes Martine would open her mouth to say something and suddenly stop, embarrassed.

'What were you going to say?'

'Nothing . . .'

Because she suddenly realized that the words she was on the point of uttering were the kind that would risk awakening my phantoms. And they might be the most innocent words in the world, such as, for instance, the name of a street, the Rue de Berry, where it seems there is a certain kind of hotel. I've never taken that street again. Like the theatre in Paris we dared not mention because of what had happened there one evening in a box, a few weeks before she left for Nantes and La Roche.

There were certain taxis of a particular colour, more numerous, alas, than any others, the very sight of which evoked the most loathsome images.

Now do you understand why our conversations sometimes resembled the gait of certain sick people, who know that a sudden movement may prove fatal? It is said that they are walking on eggs. We too were walking on eggs.

Not always, for in that case our life would not have been what it was. We had long carefree periods of pure joy. Martine, like many people who have learned to fear life, was superstitious and, if the day began too gaily, I could feel her uneasiness no matter how hard she tried to hide it.

I spent my time wrestling with her fear, annihilating her fear. I succeeded in delivering her from most of her nightmares. I made her happy. I know it. I insist on that. I forbid anyone, anyone at all, to contradict me on that score.

She was happy with me, is that clear?

And because she was happy and because she was not used to being happy she sometimes trembled.

At La Roche-sur-Yon she was afraid of Armande, of my mother and my daughters, of my friends, of everything that had made up my life until then.

At Issy-les-Moulineaux she was afraid at first of a kind of life which she thought might very well discourage me.

Of these fears, and others besides, I cured her.

But there still remained our phantoms, the ones I had taken from her, of which I had relieved her, and against which she watched me struggling.

There remained my suffering which would suddenly pierce me with so sharp a pain that I was completely disfigured by it, and just when we least expected it, when we thought ourselves out of danger, would in a matter of seconds drive me completely out of my mind.

She knew very well, you may rest assured, that it wasn't she whom I hated, that it wasn't against her that my fists were raised. She humbled herself, a humility I could never have imagined.

One detail, your Honour. The first time, instinctively, she had put her arm up in front of her face to ward off the blows. That gesture, God knows, why, redoubled my rage. And because she was aware of this, she would now wait motionless, without a quiver of her face, keeping her lips from trembling, though all her flesh recoiled in horror.

I beat her. I don't apologize. I ask no one's pardon. The only one whose pardon I might ask is Martine. And Martine doesn't need it because she knows.

I beat her in our little car, one afternoon, as we were going along the Seine ... Another time, at the cinema, and we had to leave, for otherwise I should have been massacred by our indignant neighbours ...

I have often tried to analyse what took place in me at such moments. Today I think that I am lucid enough to answer. You see, it didn't matter how much she had changed – I mean physically changed – for she had been completely transformed in a few months, there were still moments when nothing could keep me from recognizing a trait, a mannerism, an expression of the other Martine.

It would only happen when I looked at her in a certain way. And I only looked at her like that when, because of an unexpected incident, because of a word, an image, I thought of her past.

Wait! It's the word 'image' which is, undoubtedly, the key. I was able, alas, to call up without wanting to an image as distinct as a photograph, and that image would quite naturally superimpose itself on the Martine before me.

From that instant, I believed in nothing any longer. I believed in nothing, your Honour, not even in her. Not even in myself. I was submerged by an immeasurable disgust. It wasn't possible. We'd been fooled. We'd been robbed. I didn't want to. I . . .

Then I'd strike her. It was the only way. She knew it so well that she desired it, she almost invited me to do it, so that I might be more quickly delivered.

I am not mad, I am not ill. We were not ill, either of us. Were we aiming too high, were we aspiring to a love forbidden to men?

But then why, can you tell me, if it is forbidden on pain of death, why has this desire been planted in the very depth of our being?

We were honest. We did our best. We never tried to cheat.

'I am going to kill her . . .'

I did not believe it when these words kept coming back like a refrain, they didn't frighten me.

I can guess what you are thinking. It is ridiculous. Some day, you will perhaps learn that it is more difficult to kill than to get oneself killed. And even more difficult to live for months with the idea that you are going to kill the only person in the world you love.

But that's what I did. In the beginning it was vague, like the premonitory signs of a disease which begins with random discomforts, pains one cannot quite locate. I have seen patients who, speaking of a pain they felt in their chests at certain moments, indicate the wrong side.

Night after night in our bedroom at Issy-les-Moulineaux I would unconsciously attempt a treatment. I qustioned her on the child Martine, whom the Martine I loved was growing to resemble more and more each day.

We had not had time to change the wallpapers, which were covered with fantastic flowers in the worst modernistic taste. The armchair I used to sit in after putting on my dressing-gown was modernistic too and upholstered in a poisonous green velvet. The standing lamp, as well, was hideous, but we never noticed. We made no attempt to modify the frame of our daily life, so little did such things count for us.

She talked. There are names, first names which have become as familiar to me as those of the famous men of history. One of her childhood friends, for example, a certain Olga, returned to the stage every evening and played the role of villainess.

I know all Olga's perfidies, at the convent, then in society when the little girls, grown up, were taken to parties. I know all my Martine's humiliations and all her most outlandish dreams. I know her uncles, aunts, cousins, but what I know best of all is her own face becoming transformed as she spoke.

'Listen, my darling . . .'

She always gave a start when she felt that I was going to announce any news, like my mother who could never open a telegram without trembling. She was not afraid of blows, but the unknown terrified her because for her the unknown had always been translated into some evil. She would look at me with an anxiety she did her best to conceal. She knew that fear was forbidden her. It was one of our taboos.

'We are going to take a few day's vacation . . .'

She grew pale. She thought of Armande, of my daughters. She was always dreading, from the very first day, the nostalgia I might feel for La Roche and my family.

But I was smiling, proud of my idea.

'We'll spend them in your native city, in Liège . . .'

We went. A pilgrimage. And I had, moreover, the hope of leaving behind me when I left some of my phantoms for ever.

All right, I'll be even more frank and more blunt. I felt that I had to get possession of her childhood, for I was jealous of her childhood too.

This trip made her even dearer to me because more human.

People say:

'I was born in such and such a city, my parents did so and so . . .'

All that she had told me was like a novel for young girls, and I went there to get at the truth, which turned out to be not so very different. I saw the big house, Rue Hors-Château, which she had so often described, and its famous porch with the forged iron hand-rail. I listened to people telling me about her family in just the same terms she herself employed, an old family, almost patrician, which had been gradually going downhill.

I even went to see the office of her father, who at the time of his death was secretary of the provincial government.

I saw her mother, her two married sisters, the children of one of them.

I saw the streets where she used to walk with a school bag in her hand, the shop windows against which she had glued her little red nose, nipped by the frost, the motion picture theatre where she had seen her first film and the pastry shop where the Sunday cakes were purchased. I saw her classroom and the nuns who remembered her.

I understood her better. Above all I found out that I had not been mistaken, that she had not lied, that the miracle of Nantes – there's no other word – had given me an insight into all those things in her which made her my wife today.

Yet, even at Liège, your Honour, my phantoms followed me. A young man, somewhere in a café in the centre of the city where we were listening to the music, came gaily up to our table and called her by her first name.

That was enough.

The more she was mine, the more I felt that she was mine, the more I judged her worthy to be mine – I do hope that you will not see conceit in this word, which in my mind has no such connotation, for I too am humble, and I loved her as humbly as she loved me – as I say, the more she was mine the more I felt the need of absorbing her in even greater measure.

To absorb her. As I, for my part, would have liked to be wholly melted into her.

I was jealous of her mother, jealous of her little nephew who is nine years old, jealous of an old man we went to see in his little sweet shop, who had known her as a youngster, and who still remembered her tastes. He did, however, give me a tiny thrill of pleasure when, after a short hesitation, he called her:

'Mme Martine . . .'

You see, I would have to take you through all the stages, one by one, that we ourselves passed through. Spring went. Summer came. The flowers in the Paris squares changed many times, our sombre suburb brightened, urchins and men in bathing trunks swarmed along the banks of the Seine, while we, at every turn of the road, found still another stage to be travelled.

Her flesh had soon become as obedient as her mind. We reached and ventured on the stage of silence. We could now read side by side in our bed.

We were able, with due precaution and with a show of courage, to cross certain forbidden neighbourhoods.

'You'll see, Martine, the day will come when there won't be a single phantom left.'

They came less and less often. We went together to see my daughters at Sables d'Olonne, where Armande had taken a villa. Martine waited for me in the car.

Looking out of the open window, Armande said:

'You didn't come alone?'

'No.'

Quite simply, your Honour, because it was simple.

'Your daughters are on the beach.'

'I'll go and see them there.'

'With her?'

'Yes.'

And, as I declined her invitation to lunch:

'Is she jealous?'

It was better to say nothing. I remained silent.

'Are you happy?'

She shook her head gloomily, with a touch of sadness, and sighed:

'Ah, well . . .'

How could I make her understand that one can be happy and still suffer? Are they not two words which go quite naturally together, and had I ever suffered, really suffered, until Martine gave me the revelation of happiness?

As I left, I very nearly said aloud:

'I am going to kill her.'

So that she would understand even less! As though I had wanted my little vengeance!

We chattered with my daughters on the beach, Martine and I. I saw Mama, who was sitting on the sand knitting. She behaved very well, she offered no criticism, and when we left, holding out her hand she said very nicely:

'Goodbye, Mademoiselle . . .'

I could swear that she too was on the point of saying Madame. But did not dare.

There was no reproach, only a slight apprehension, in the glances she gave me, surreptitiously as was her wont.

And yet I was happy, I have never been so happy in my life, Martine and I were happy enough to shout it from the house tops.

It was the third of September, a Sunday. I know the effect of that date on you. Don't worry, I am calm.

The weather was soft and muggy, if you remember. It was no longer summer and it was not yet winter. For days the sky was grey, that grey which is both dull and luminous and that has always depressed me. Many people, especially in the poorer suburbs like ours, had already returned from vacation or had never gone away.

We had a maid now, for the last three days, a young girl from Picardy, who came to us direct from the country. She was sixteen and her figure was still shapeless, and she looked like a big rag doll. Her skin was always red and shiny and, in her pink dress, comically bulging, with her bare legs, her bare feet in felt slippers, her hair always dishevelled, she looked, in our little apartment where she kept bumping into the furniture, as if she were just going to milk the cows.

I am never able to stay in bed after a certain hour. I got up quietly and Martine, just as she used to with her father, held out her arms and demanded, without opening her eyes:

'A big hug . . .'

That meant I was to hold her tight against my breast until I squeezed all the breath out of her; then she was satisfied.

All our Sunday mornings were exactly alike. They were not mine, they were Martine's. She was a little city girl, while I, peasant that I am, had always risen with the dawn.

In her eyes the worst instrument of torture ever invented was the alarm clock, with its brutal, piercing bell.

'Even when I was a little girl and had to get up to go to school . . .'

Later, she had to get up to go to work. She would employ little stratagems. She would set the clock ten minutes fast intentionally, so she could linger a little longer in bed.

And yet, for all those last months, every morning she would get up before me in order to bring me my first cup of coffee in bed because I had once told her that that is what my mother had always done.

She was not, after all, a girl for the morning. It took her a long time after she was up to return to the waking world. It used to amuse me to see her coming and going in her pyjamas, her walk a little unsteady, her face still puffed up with sleep. Sometimes I would burst out laughing.

'What's the weather today?'

'Nothing . . .'

Every Sunday I offered her what she called the ideal morning. She would sleep late, until about ten o'clock, and it was my turn then to bring her her coffee. Drinking it in bed, she would light her first cigarette, for that was the only thing I had not had the heart to make her give up. She had suggested it. She would have done it. But at least it was no longer that constant necessity it had once been. Nor a pose.

She would turn on the radio and much later she would finally inquire:

'What's the weather today?'

We would plan not to have any plans so that this day of rest should be free for improvisation. And often, indeed, we did nothing at all.

I remember on that particular Sunday, I stayed for a long time looking out of the living-room window. I still see a family waiting for the bus, each one of its members – there were seven of them, mother, father, boys, and girls – carrying a fishing-rod.

A band went by, brass instruments following behind a banner resplendent with gold fringe, a music club of some sort, with young men wearing arm bands making a great hullabaloo as they marched along the pavements. People in the houses across the street were leaning out of the windows and I could hear the muffled sound of their radios.

When I went downstairs, a little before ten o'clock, she was still in bed. As an exception, I had given an appointment to a patient who required a treatment I had not time to give him during the week, since it took almost an hour. He was a foreman about fifty years old, an excellent fellow, conscientious in the extreme.

He was waiting for me at the door. We went into my office, and he began undressing at once. I washed my hands again, put on my hospital coat. Everything was so calm it was as though life was suspended in the world.

Did the colour of the sky have something to do with it? It was one of those days, your Honour – they are always Sundays – when one is capable of thinking of nothing.

I was thinking of nothing. My patient kept talking in a monotonous voice to keep up his courage, for the treatment was rather painful. Then he would stop, try to suppress a groan and hasten to say:

'Go on, Doctor . . . it's nothing . . .'

He got dressed again and held out his hand when he was ready to leave. We went out together and I locked up my shop-like office. I looked up, thinking that Martine might, by chance, be at the window. I walked to the corner to buy a paper. They were sold in a little bar. I had a medicinal after-taste in my mouth and drank a vermouth at the bar.

I went slowly upstairs to the apartment. I opened the door. Did I make less noise than usual? Martine and the maid, who was called Elise, were together in the kitchen and they were laughing at the top of their lungs.

I smiled. I was happy. I went towards the kitchen and saw them. Elise was standing at the sink preparing vegetables, and Martine, in her dressing-gown, was seated with her elbows on the table, her hair dishevelled, a cigarette in her mouth.

I have rarely felt such tenderness for her. You see, I had just stumbled on another side of her nature I didn't know and which delighted me.

I like people who can enjoy themselves with their maids, especially with little peasant girls like Elise. And I knew that is was not out of condescension that she was there, like so many ladies of the house. I could tell that from their voices and their laughter.

While I was downstairs there they were, two youngsters who had met one lazy Sunday morning and started chattering.

About what? I didn't try find out. They were laughing over nonsensical nothings, I am sure, things that can't be explained, that a man can never understand.

She was disconcerted, seeing me appear.

'You were there? Elise and I were telling each other stories. . . . What is it?'

'Nothing . . .'

'Yes . . . There's something . . . Come . . .'

She rose, uneasy, and led me into our bedroom.

'You are angry?'

'Of course not.'

'You are sad?'

'I swear . . .'

I was neither the one nor the other. I was moved, idiotically perhaps, I was much more moved than I cared to appear or to admit to myself.

Even today it would be difficult for me to say just why. Perhaps because that morning, involuntarily, without any precise reason, I felt that I was reaching the maximum of my love, the maximum of understanding that one human being can have of another.

You see, I felt so sure that I understood her! She was so fresh, so pure, this child who was laughing in the kitchen with our little peasant girl . . .

Then, perfidiously, another sentiment insinuated itself – a vague distress, alas, familiar to me, and against which I should have reacted at once.

She had understood. That is why she had taken me into the bedroom. That is why she was waiting.

Why she was waiting for me to strike. It would have been better. But several weeks before I had sworn to myself that I would never give way to my loathsome rages again.

A few days earlier, on Wednesday, coming home arm in arm from our local cinema, I had pointed out to her, not without pride:

'You see . . . It is already three weeks . . .'

'Yes . . .'

She knew what I meant. She was not as optimistic as I was.

'At first it was four or five days . . . Then once a week or every two weeks . . .'

Then jokingly:

'When it is only every six months . . .'

She had pressed her thigh tighter against mine. It was one of our pleasures to walk that way, thigh to thigh, in the evenings, when the pavements were deserted, as though we were a single moving body.

I did not strike her that Sunday morning because I was too deeply moved, because the phantoms were too vague, because, at first and for many a long hour afterwards, no brutal images appeared.

'Are you annoyed because I am not dressed yet?'

'Of course not . . .'

There was nothing. Why then was she so uneasy? She continued to be uneasy all the rest of the day. We had luncheon together near the open window.

'What would you like to do?'

'I don't know. Anything you like.'

'How about going to the Vincennes Zoo?'

She had never been there. She knew animals only from having seen a few in passing circuses.

We went. The same luminous veil was still stretched across the sky and it just happened to be the sort of light that does not cast shadows. The place was crowded. Cakes, ice cream cones, peanuts were being sold everywhere. We lingered for a long time in front of the cages, the bears' pit, the monkey house.

'Look, Charles . . .'

And I can still see them, two chimpanzees, the male and the female, standing there in an embrace, looking at the crowd, looking, your Honour, the way I looked at all of you in the courtroom during the trial.

It was the male who, in a gesture both gentle and protective, had put his long arm round the female.

'Charles . . .'

Yes, I know. It is in just about the same position, isn't it, Martine, that we fall asleep every night? We were not in a cage but we were perhaps just as frightened of what lay beyond our invisible bars, and to reassure you I drew you closer.

I was suddenly sad. It seemed to me . . . I can still see the swarming crowd in the Zoo, those thousands of families, those children, whose parents were buying them chocolates and red balloons, those bands of boisterous young men, those lovers filching flowers from the flower borders; I still hear that muffled tramping of a crowd, and I see the two of us, I feel the two of us, my throat tight for no apparent reason, while she murmurs:

'Let's go back to see them, shall we?'

The two monkeys, our two monkeys.

Then we walked around for a while longer in the dust until its taste was in our mouths. We went back to our car and I thought:

'If . . .'

If she had been only herself, your Honour, if she had never been other than the one I had come upon in the kitchen that morning, if she had been only, if we had both been only like that male and female whom we had, each of us, without any prompting from the other, at the same moment, suddenly envied! . . .

'Do you want to have dinner at home?'

'Just as you like. Elise is out, but there is plenty of food in the house.'

I preferred to eat in a restaurant. I was on edge, uneasy. I felt that the phantoms were there, close by, waiting for a chance to leap at my throat.

Abruptly I asked:

'What did you used to do Sundays?'

She couldn't possibly misunderstand. She knew what period of her life I meant. She couldn't answer. She stammered:

'I was bored . . .'

It wasn't true. She was perhaps bored deep down in herself, but she craved pleasure and would go anywhere to find it . . .

I rose from the table before the end of the meal. Night was falling lazily, too slowly to suit me.

'Let's go home . . .'

I wanted to drive. I never opened my mouth the whole way. I kept repeating to myself:

'You mustn't . . .'

And I was still only thinking of the blows.

'She hasn't deserved that ... She's a poor little girl ...'

Of course! Of course! I know! Who could know it better than I? Who? Tell me that!

I put my hand on her hand just as we were coming to Issy.

'Don't be afraid ...'

'I'm not afraid ...'

I should have struck her. There was still time. We were still connected, more or less, with the outside world. There were streets, pavements, people walking, others sitting on chairs in front of their doors. There were lights struggling against the false daylight of evening. There was the Seine with its drowsing barges.

Just as I was putting the key in the lock I almost said:

'Let's not go in ...'

And yet I knew nothing. I had no premonition. I had never loved her so much. It wasn't possible – for God's sake, won't you understand – that she ... she ...

I opened the door and she went in. And everything was settled at that moment. I had a few seconds to turn back. She, too, had had time to elude her destiny, to elude me.

I see once more the nape of her neck as I turned on the light switch, the nape of her neck as I had seen it that first day in front of the ticket office of the station at Nantes, with those little curling tendrils of hair.

'Do you want to go to bed right away?'

I said yes.

What was wrong with us that evening and why did so many things catch us in the throat?

I went to get her glass of milk. Every night in bed,

after we had loved each other, she would always drink a glass of milk.

And she drank it that night, the night of Sunday, the third of September. That means we had possessed each other, that she had had time afterwards slowly to sip her milk, sitting up in bed.

I had not struck her. I had driven away the phantoms.

'Good night, Charles . . .'

'Good night, Martine . . .'

We would always repeat those words two or three times in a particular tone of voice, like an incantation:

'Good night, Charles . . .'

'Good night, Martine . . .'

Her head sought its place in the hollow of my shoulder and she gave a little sigh, her little nightly sigh, she stammered, as she did every evening before falling asleep:

'It really isn't Christian . . .'

Then the phantoms came, the most hideous, the most loathsome ones, and it was too late – and they knew it – for me to defend myself.

Martine was asleep. Or else she pretended to be asleep to quiet me.

Slowly, my hand crept up along her thigh, caressing her smooth skin, her smooth, smooth skin, followed the curve of her waist and stopped as it passed over the firm softness of a breast.

Images, more images, other hands, other caresses . . .

The roundness of a shoulder where the skin is smoothest, then a warm hollow, the neck . . .

I knew very well, yes, I knew it was too late. All the phantoms were there, the other Martine was there, the one they had sullied, all of them, the one who had let herself be sullied with a sort of frenzy . . .

And must my own Martine, the one who was still laughing so innocently that morning with our little maid, must she suffer for it eternally? Must we, both of us, suffer to the end of our days?

Wasn't it necessary to deliver us, to deliver her from all her fears, from all her shame?

It was not dark. It was never completely dark in our room at Issy, because there were only ecru linen curtains at the windows and because a street-lamp stood directly opposite.

I could see her. I did see her. I could see my hand about her neck, and I pressed, your Honour, brutally. I saw her eyes open, I saw her first look, which was a look of terror; then immediately another, a look of resignation and deliverance, a look of love.

I pressed. These were my fingers that were choking her. I couldn't do otherwise. I kept crying to her:

'Forgive me, Martine . . .'

And I felt that she was encouraging me, that she wished it, that she had always foreseen this moment, *that it was the only way out.*

I had to kill the Other, once and for all, so that my Martine could live at last.

I killed the Other. Fully conscious of what I was doing. You see now that there was premeditation, that there had to be premeditation, otherwise the act would have been absurd.

I killed her that she might live, and our eyes continued to embrace to the very end.

To the very end, your Honour. After that our immobility, hers and mine, was identical. My hand was still round her neck, and it stayed there for a long time.

I closed her eyes. I kissed them. I rose, staggering,

and I am not sure what I would have done if, at that moment, I had not heard a key turning in the lock. It was Élise coming home.

You heard what she said, both in court and in your office. She did nothing but repeat:

'Monsieur was very calm, but he didn't seem like an ordinary man . . .'

I said to her:

'Get the police . . .'

I never thought of the telephone. I waited for a long time sitting on the edge of the bed.

And it was during those moments that I realized one thing: that I would have to live, for, so long as I lived, my Martine would live.

She was in me. I bore her within me as she had borne me. The Other was dead, for ever, but as long as there was one human being, myself, to keep the real Martine in him, the real Martine would continue to exist.

Wasn't that why I had killed the Other?

That, your Honour, is why I have lived, why I endured the trial, that is why I didn't want your pity, yours or anybody's, or all those tricks that might have got me acquitted. That is why I don't want to be pronounced mad, or irresponsible.

For Martine.

For the real Martine.

So that I shall really have delivered her. So that our love may live, and it is only in me that it can live.

I am not mad. I am just a man, a man like other men, but a man who has loved, who knows what love is.

I shall live in her, with her, for her, as long as I possibly can, and if I imposed upon myself this waiting, if I inflicted on myself that sort of circus which was called a trial, it was so that she, no matter what the cost, may continue to live in someone.

If I am writing you this long letter, it is so that the day I finally weigh anchor, someone will succeed to our heritage, so that my Martine and her love will never wholly die.

We went as far as it was possible to go. We did all we possibly could.

We wanted the totality of love.

Goodbye, your Honour.

Chapter Eleven

The very day that examining magistrate Coméliau, 22 bis Rue de Seine, Paris, received this letter, the newspaper announced that Dr Charles Alavoine, born at Bourgneuf in the Vendée, had committed suicide in the infirmary of the prison, under rather mysterious circumstances.

'In deference to his past life and his profession, and considering his calmness and what the chief doctor of the prison calls his good humour, he was sometimes left alone for a few moments in the infirmary where he was receiving medical attention.

'He had access, in this way, to the cabinet where toxic drugs are kept and was able to poison himself.

'An inquiry has been opened.'

LIMERICK
COUNTY LIBRARY

TITLES IN SERIES

J.R. ACKERLEY Hindoo Holiday
J.R. ACKERLEY My Dog Tulip
J.R. ACKERLEY My Father and Myself
J.R. ACKERLEY We Think the World of You
HENRY ADAMS The Jeffersonian Transformation
CÉLESTE ALBARET Monsieur Proust
DANTE ALIGHIERI The Inferno
DANTE ALIGHIERI The New Life
WILLIAM ATTAWAY Blood on the Forge
W.H. AUDEN (EDITOR) The Living Thoughts of Kierkegaard
W.H. AUDEN W.H. Auden's Book of Light Verse
ERICH AUERBACH Dante: Poet of the Secular World
DOROTHY BAKER Cassandra at the Wedding
J.A. BAKER The Peregrine
HONORÉ DE BALZAC The Unknown Masterpiece *and* Gambara
MAX BEERBOHM Seven Men
STEPHEN BENATAR Wish Her Safe at Home
FRANS G. BENGTSSON The Long Ships
ALEXANDER BERKMAN Prison Memoirs of an Anarchist
GEORGES BERNANOS Mouchette
ADOLFO BIOY CASARES Asleep in the Sun
ADOLFO BIOY CASARES The Invention of Morel
CAROLINE BLACKWOOD Corrigan
CAROLINE BLACKWOOD Great Granny Webster
NICOLAS BOUVIER The Way of the World
MALCOLM BRALY On the Yard
MILLEN BRAND The Outward Room
JOHN HORNE BURNS The Gallery
ROBERT BURTON The Anatomy of Melancholy
CAMARA LAYE The Radiance of the King
GIROLAMO CARDANO The Book of My Life
DON CARPENTER Hard Rain Falling
J.L. CARR A Month in the Country
BLAISE CENDRARS Moravagine
EILEEN CHANG Love in a Fallen City
UPAMANYU CHATTERJEE English, August: An Indian Story
NIRAD C. CHAUDHURI The Autobiography of an Unknown Indian
ANTON CHEKHOV Peasants and Other Stories
RICHARD COBB Paris and Elsewhere
COLETTE The Pure and the Impure
JOHN COLLIER Fancies and Goodnights
CARLO COLLODI The Adventures of Pinocchio
IVY COMPTON-BURNETT A House and Its Head
IVY COMPTON-BURNETT Manservant and Maidservant
BARBARA COMYNS The Vet's Daughter
EVAN S. CONNELL The Diary of a Rapist
ALBERT COSSERY The Jokers
HAROLD CRUSE The Crisis of the Negro Intellectual
ASTOLPHE DE CUSTINE Letters from Russia